# THE GUNSMITH

# 401

## New Mexico Powder Keg

**Books by J.R. Roberts**
**(Robert J. Randisi)**

*The Gunsmith* series

*Gunsmith Giant* series

*Lady Gunsmith* series

*Angel Eyes* series

*Tracker* series

*Mountain Jack Pike* series


**COMING SOON!**
**The Gunsmith**
402 – Ransom for a Gunsmith


**For more information**
**visit:** www.SpeakingVolumes.us

# THE GUNSMITH

# 401

## New Mexico Powder Keg

J.R. Roberts

SPEAKING VOLUMES, LLC
NAPLES, FLORIDA
2024

New Mexico Powder Keg



*New Mexico Powder Keg* is a work of historical fiction. Many of the important historical events, figures, and locations are as accurately portrayed as possible. In keeping with a work of fiction, various events and occurrences were invented by the author.

ISBN 979-8-89022-183-4

# Chapter One



*West Texas*

When Clint Adams rode into Texas from Oklahoma, his intent had been to visit some old friends, toss back a few beers and kick up his heels for a while. That jovial mood had followed him like fragrant smoke around a cooking fire and lasted almost as long. He'd made camp, fallen asleep while counting the stars and woke up with his supper still warm in his belly.

It wasn't unusual for Clint's slumber to be interrupted unexpectedly. Any man who lived his life by the gun had his share of ghosts to contend with. The faces of all those dead men didn't fade like any other memory. They lingered and grew silent at times, only to come back and howl in the dark at others. On this occasion, Clint twitched and reached for his modified Colt, fully expecting to hear the remnant of some old nightmare rattling around in the back of his mind.

There were no ghosts vying for his attention and no echoes of gunfire from one of the many times in his past when Clint had nearly met his maker. For a moment, Clint wondered if the twitch had merely been the result of gobbling down that last bit of pork and beans from dinner he should have tossed aside. Rather than sit up or stretch his legs, he kept still and waited.

Another few seconds passed and then he heard it.

Rustling.

It came from nearby and was just loud enough to catch his attention. More than that, it sounded as if whatever was creating the sound was trying not to be heard. When animals moved like that, they did so gracefully and easily. It was instinct. When men moved with the same intentions, it was more deliberate. The sound Clint heard was the latter. He'd had more than enough people try to sneak up on him over the years to know that sound better than almost any other.

His hand eased a bit closer to his holstered pistol while his eyes searched the shadows at the edge of his campfire for any hint of movement. He quickly picked out two shadows that hadn't been there when he'd rested his head upon his bedroll earlier that night. As his fingers curled around the grip of his Colt, Clint listened to every rustle in the breeze and stared through the slits of his eyelids at the men hunkered down over his saddlebags.

Since it seemed the intruders weren't aware that he was awake, Clint used that to his advantage and rolled away from his resting spot. Almost immediately, a shot blasted through the chilly air and a piece of lead scorched through the spot that Clint had just vacated. Dirt from the impact was still flying in all directions when Clint answered back with a shot of his own.

The Colt bucked against his palm, spitting its fiery retort in the direction of the sparks that had accompanied the first shot that had been sent his way. Knowing he most likely hadn't hit anything, Clint scrambled to his feet so he could move away from the dim light of the dying fire.

"He's awake!" a man said from the direction of the first gunshot.

One of the shadows Clint had picked out from the darkness replied, "I can see that! Put him down, fer chrissakes!"

A second plume of sparks erupted from nearby, briefly illuminating the man who'd set this fight into motion. He was a skinny fellow with a long face covered in stubble and dirt. Clint stayed low and took a few quick steps before planting his feet and squeezing off another shot. While his first bullet had been meant to buy him some time, the second wasn't about to be wasted. Keeping steady even as a panicked shot was fired in his direction, Clint took aim to send his round straight through the skinny man's chest.

As one of the intruders spun on a heel and fell over after being hit, the other two answered back by pulling their triggers again and again. One of them proved to be smarter than the rest by hurrying to get behind solid cover. That left one of the strangers in the open and he took a rushed shot while wailing in a voice that sounded like rusty iron being dragged over dry slate.

"Where the hell you goin', Laird?" the stranger said as he pulled his trigger one more time.

"Leave my property where you found it," Clint announced, "or I'll drop you right beside it."

The man with the grating voice was short in height and thick around the middle. For a moment, he looked around as if he didn't realize he was the one still holding Clint's saddlebags in one hand. Tightening his grip on the hand tooled leather, he held the bags close and said, "You want your things? Come and get 'em!"

"Suit yourself," Clint replied as he stood up.

Obviously not accustomed to anyone calling him on that particular taunt, the man holding Clint's saddlebags gawked at him and took a step back. To his right, the third man poked his head up from behind the boulder he'd found and sighted along the top of his pistol.

Both of the remaining intruders moved at the same time. Clint was watching them carefully, waiting for a juicy target to present itself. When one of the men fumbled to thumb back the hammer of his pistol while the other straightened his arm to take a more careful shot, Clint's choice was practically made for him.

Clint took half of a second to steady his arm before squeezing his trigger. As soon as the gun went off, he immediately shifted his aim to the next target in line and fired again. Both shots came in quick succession and when they were done, the crack from the pistol's barrel rolled through the air to disperse into the night like so much thunder.

The intruder that had been hunkering behind a rock had been the recipient of the first of those last two shots. He flopped backward to land sprawled on the ground, his brains leaking out through the hole that had been freshly drilled through his skull. The man who'd tried to lay claim to Clint's saddlebag gnashed his teeth and slowly wilted as he reached down to his right leg. Blood from the wound he'd just received glistened in the dim moonlight as the pain slowly seeped in.

Clint was about to tell him to drop his gun, but the pistol slipped from the intruder's hand to land heavily at his feet. As he stepped forward, Clint looked around for any other shadows that might have been trying to creep in on him. Although he couldn't find any other shapes in the darkness, he quickly realized one shape wasn't where it should have been.

Eclipse, Clint's Darley Arabian stallion, was gone.

# Chapter Two

For the first couple of minutes, Clint didn't speak. He kept himself busy first by dragging the wounded man closer to the campfire and then wrapping him up in rope that had been coiled near the saddle that was laying on the ground. He did these things slowly and deliberately, without responding in the slightest to anything the other man said. And that man did say an awful lot.

"This was just a mistake," the man said. "Just a big mistake. We . . . we thought you was someone else. Yeah! It was supposed to be a joke. All right . . . well . . . not a joke so much as a . . ."

Clint stopped what he was doing and glared intently at him.

"It's like I said," the man continued in a meeker tone. "Just a mistake. No harm done. Leastways, not to you."

Now that the man was getting some wind back into his sail, Clint picked up his pace a bit. If the man so much as twitched the wrong way, Clint was prepared to draw his Colt and finish the job he'd started. It turned out that all he really needed to do was cinch in the ropes around the man's legs to put him back in his place. Once the weathered binding scraped against the man's bullet wound, he was too busy squirming to do much else.

"You killed two men here tonight," the prisoner said. "Let me go and we'll call it even. If you push me, mister, I warn you I can make things pretty damn rough!"

The prisoner's gun was still where it had landed when he'd dropped it. Just to make sure he wasn't in for any surprises, Clint patted him down for any other weapons. All he found was a hunting knife hanging from his belt and a flat rock in his pocket. Clint removed both, palming the rock in his left hand and sending the knife whistling through the air with a snap of his right.

The blade spun one complete rotation before digging into the dirt squarely between the prisoner's legs. Having a close call with that much sharpened steel was more than enough to shut him up.

"What's your name?" Clint asked.

Recoiling as if he'd heard a voice come from the trunk of a petrified tree, the prisoner replied, "Sven. Svenson."

Since he didn't give a damn if the other man had stuttered or just possessed a boring name, Clint said, "All right, Sven. Now tell me where to find my horse."

"I . . . I don't . . ."

"And before you try to pass yourself off as some innocent bystander, remember I saw you shooting at me while you tried stealing my saddlebags."

Suddenly, Sven's face brightened. "That's right! That's all I meant to do. I swear! Just take some supplies. I didn't have no part in taking a horse. That's a hangin' offense."

Clint stood up so he loomed over the man. Placing his hand upon the Colt at his side, he said, "Being hung is the least of your worries right now, Sven."

"How do you know your horse was taken? Maybe he just ran off."

"Honestly," Clint replied dryly. "That's the story you're hitching your ride to?"

"I'm here and your horse ain't. What do you want from me?"

"You can start by telling me where to find those men you're riding with." Clint glanced over to the nearest carcass and added, "Or . . . the men you were riding with."

Looking back and forth from the gun at Clint's side to the blade that had been stuck between his legs, Sven acquired a distinct desperation in his eye. "I just signed on with them a week ago," he sighed. "Honest."

"Who are they?"

"That one over there," Sven said while nodding in the direction of the man who'd fired the first shot, "was Laird. A killer from Missouri."

"And the other one?"

"I just knew him as Cort."

"What's his last name?" Clint asked.

Sven shook his head. "We didn't give no last names. Didn't need them or want 'em. We were just put together for this one job for a quick payday and then it was to be on to the next. I didn't intend on getting to know any of these men very much at all until I worked with them some more and that's the truth, mister."

Clint had plenty of experience in reading the truth in other people. While it wasn't an exact science by any stretch of the imagination, he had enough confidence to know that the man in front of him now was too tired and scared to tell a convincing lie. Besides that, there was something else that interested him even more. "Who put you three together?"

Like any drowning rat, Sven was all too happy to grab on to the first lifeline that was tossed his way. His eyes widened and he said, "Andy Bennelli is the man's name!"

"Where can I find him?"

"Just across the border in New Mexico. I'll take you straight to him. He'll have your horse, mister. I can get it back for you without a hitch."

"I'll get him back all right," Clint snarled.

Sven was grinning now. "That's right. I guarantee it. First, my leg will need tending. Seeing as how it was shot and all."

The wound on Sven's leg was nothing serious, which was exactly what Clint had intended. After just a few seconds of observing the cowardly sheen in the man's eyes, he'd known that if anyone was going to spill his guts about what had happened, it would be Sven. He hadn't expected it to be a complicated story and he was right about that. Unfortunately, Eclipse was already gone by the time Clint had woken up and it was too dark to track the stallion right away. The three men he'd caught red-handed hadn't been much, but whoever had gotten Eclipse was slicker than pond scum.

Sven's face was turning paler by the moment and blood was still seeping from his leg. Grudgingly, Clint told him, "I'll bind that wound and stop the bleeding."

"Thanks, mister. Don't worry about me tryin' nothin' either. Now that we're seeing eye to eye . . ."

"I'm not worried," Clint said as his hand snapped out to crack the butt of his Colt against Sven's temple. Once the thief was unconscious, it was a simple matter to keep him from bleeding out. After all, Sven still had work to do.

# Chapter Three

There wasn't much of a chance that Clint would get any sleep that night. He may have nodded off once or twice for a few minutes here and there, but he wasn't about to relax enough to do much more than that. His only concern was waiting for daybreak so he could get a jump on finding Eclipse. Knowing the stallion as well as he did, Clint was sure whoever had taken him wasn't having an easy time of it.

"Hold on, boy," he said to himself as the first rays of dawn brightened the eastern horizon. "I'm coming."

The first thing he did when he was able to see more than a few feet in front of him was to check the ground for tracks. They were easy enough to find in the dry Texas dirt. Clint smirked when he found deeper gouges in the earth along with sharp, jagged scrapes in some parts of the terrain where rocks were close to the surface. Those, along with the erratic prints left behind by a set of boots shuffling around the hoof marks told Clint a struggle between man and beast had taken place there.

Seeing that the tracks clearly led toward the West, Clint surveyed his surroundings even further. Three horses were tethered a short distance away, just far enough for them to go unnoticed in the dark of night. He went to the horses, gathered them up and brought them back to his camp. By the time he returned, Sven was awake.

"Holy hell," the thief grunted. "I got a damn bad headache." He squinted, strained at the ropes binding him and then winced. "Awww shit. I remember now. You bushwhacked me when I wasn't lookin'."

"And I recall you taking a shot or two at me while your partners tried to rob me blind."

"Yeah. There was that, I suppose."

"Not to mention that those same men also tried shooting me dead."

Sven showed Clint a crooked grin. "All right, then. I suppose we're even, huh?"

"Not by a stretch."

When Clint loaded Sven onto one of the horses he'd found, he wasn't at all gentle about it. Apart from griping that he wasn't on his own horse, Sven complained about everything under the sun including an aching emptiness in his belly.

"You got some sand, I'll grant you that much," Clint mused. "After all you did, you still get around to complaining about your accommodations."

"If you're gonna kill me, then do it. If not, then at least treat me civil and give me somethin' to eat!"

Clint approached Sven who was now draped over one of the dead men's horses like a load of flour. Staring dead into his eyes, Clint said, "There's a whole lot of wiggle room between being treated civil and being dead."

Sven's imagination told him enough to make him swallow hard and cool his heels a bit.

After sifting through the saddlebags of all three horses, Clint condensed their contents into two sets of bags so he could place his own gear across the back of the horse he'd chosen to ride. It was a young mare with an easy manner that took to him more than the other two. Collecting the reins for all three animals, Clint led them away from the camp so he could follow the tracks left by the men he was hunting. Soon, he came to a conclusion.

"It was only one man that took my horse," Clint said.

"That's right," Sven replied.

"Who was it?"

Sven wasn't anxious to part with that name, but he seemed even less anxious to get on worse terms with his captor. Reluctantly, he said, "Victor Howlett."

"I've heard that name before."

"So you know I ain't lying!"

"I heard he was dead," Clint added.

Sven's spirits dropped so low that Clint could almost hear the crash. "If he is, then someone's lying and it ain't me."

"Last I heard, he was strung up in San Antonio for horse thievery."

"Oh, see there's your mistake," Sven quickly said. "He was caught in San Antone and given a date with the noose, but he slipped away before he was forced to keep it."

"Is that so?"

Sven nodded furiously. "He was busted out by the same folks he works with right now. I must'a heard the story a dozen times if I heard it once. You wanna hear the whole tale from start to finish?"

"No," Clint snapped. His instincts told him that Sven was telling the truth as far as he knew it, but having him tell his story wouldn't do much of anything other than make a lot of noise when he wanted to keep quiet. In the end, Clint hadn't heard more than a few passing rumors himself on the matter.

The tracks he was following stretched out into a pattern left behind by a horse at a full gallop. Since they were headed in a straight line for the moment, Clint decided it was time to cover some serious ground. Before saddling up, however, he took a bandanna from his saddlebag and approached Sven.

"Oh, there's no need for that," Sven said as Clint approached him with the bandanna.

Twisting the bandanna into a thick length of cotton, Clint replied, "I beg to differ."

"I'll keep quiet."

"That's right. You will."

# Chapter Four

The trail took some irregular turns that would have presented a problem for anyone trying to follow it. Even Clint might have lost it throughout the day if not for the trouble Eclipse continued to give whoever was leading him away. Every so often, the Darley Arabian would put up a fight or create some other kind of fuss that left behind plenty of scuff marks, gouges and chipped rocks for Clint to discover. When he would find one of those signs, he couldn't help but grin.

"That's a good boy," Clint said under his breath. "Not much longer now."

The further along he went, the more Clint became convinced that Sven had truly been riding with Victor Howlett. If it was another horse thief trading in on a known name, the man was doing a hell of a job of living up to Howlett's reputation. Anyone who could keep hold of Eclipse when the stallion wanted to get away was definitely someone who knew their way around a horse.

After bringing his small group to a stop on a small rise, Clint took a pair of field glasses from his saddlebag and studied the terrain ahead. Behind him, he could hear the sound of horses shifting on their hooves along with an insistent, muffled grunting. Clint was about to tell Sven to keep quiet, but then reminded himself how long it had been since he'd allowed the captured thief to stretch his legs.

As soon as the bandanna was pulled down, Sven let out a relieved sigh. "Any chance I can take a piss?" was the first thing he needed to say.

Clint pulled him down from the horse's back and shoved him toward some bushes. As Sven relieved himself, Clint asked, "how many others were riding with you?"

"Just us three and Howlett. But Victor liked to ride alone mostly. Is that Parker up ahead?"

"Who?"

"Not who. What! Parker's the name of a town. Little place with three saloons and a run-down cathouse. The lady at that cathouse serves some damn fine grub, though."

Squinting at the town in the distance, Clint did some quick figuring. He knew most of West Texas like the back of his hand. He'd heard mention of a town named Parker in these parts, but hadn't made it out there until now. From what he'd heard of the place, Parker was a little mud hole of a town that appealed to vermin like Sven and any other horse thieves who might ride with him.

"Would Howlett want to meet up with Andy Berelli in a town like that?" Clint asked.

"Bennelli," Sven corrected. "And it makes sense for him to bring a stolen animal there."

"You don't know for certain?"

"I already told you. Howlett kept to himself about damn near everything. I've made a few deals there myself, but not with Bennelli."

Clint didn't trust Sven any farther than he could toss him. He made it a habit not to trust anyone who was angling for a way to escape, kill him or both. Still, the tracks he'd been following led straight to that town and at the very least, there might be someone in Parker who either knew Howlett or had spotted Eclipse. Darley Arabians weren't exactly a common sight in any part of the country.

"You know a good place in Parker to stop for the night?" Clint asked.

Despite being carried like baggage, Sven looked genuinely pleased to be asked that question. "Why yes!" he said. "There's a great hotel on the east side of town with fair rates and soft beds."

"Great to hear it." With that, Clint steered his procession to some more promising places on the opposite end of Parker.

# Chapter Five

Jarred Hall had been in Parker for only a few hours and he was already feeling restless. There were plenty of sights and sounds to capture a man's attention in a place catering to the likes of horse thieves, stagecoach robbers or anyone else who'd ever pointed a gun at another man within the great state of Texas. But Hall wasn't paying any mind to those things when he made his way up and down one street after another.

To every smile from a working girl, he gave only a halfhearted nod.

To every threatening glare he got from an armed man, Hall responded with a stare that could send a wildcat scampering back to its den.

While most of the people he saw didn't know Hall from any other soul wandering in from the Texas plains, he knew most of them. Knowing them was how he made his living, just as being unknown to them was how he stayed alive. Navigating such treacherous waters was an art. It was a subtle mixture of knowing when to stare someone in the eyes and for precisely the right length of time before looking away. It was knowing when to keep his head down completely and allow the scarf around his neck and the brim of his hat to hide him away.

Jarred Hall's face was rougher than the road leading through that outlaw town on the Texas and New Mexico border. His nose was broken in two places. His hair grew irregularly after being shorn close to his scalp by a razor that was badly in need of sharpening. Scars cut through the flesh of his neck and chin, telling gruesome tales of encounters with the reaper himself. In a more civilized town, such markings may have been distinctive. In Parker, they labeled Jarred Hall as someone who'd earned his place on those streets. He was a man to be feared.

In any town, that was the case.

As he made his way through Parker's entertainment district, Hall kept his hand resting upon the grip of the Remington holstered at his side. The familiar weight of a .38 caliber pistol was under his right arm, but he knew better than to take comfort from such things. Nearly every man in town was armed. Any of them who weren't heeled wouldn't be alive long enough to be a problem anyhow.

As Hall passed each person on or near that street, he may not have looked at each of them directly but he saw everyone. His steps were methodical and sure, cutting a path through town like a surgeon's blade through infected flesh. There was a cathouse to his left and another a little further up the street on his right. He could smell at least one opium den and heard the warbling singing of a drunk showgirl from a distant saloon. It was early evening which meant the town was just stretching its tattered wings.

Spotting one man riding a sleek horse, Hall angled his head so most of his face was covered. When he saw the man was leading another horse by its reins, he positioned himself on the boardwalk outside one of the cathouses and waited for the rider to pass.

"Why don't you come in?" a stout redhead asked from behind him. She smelled of whiskey and the last three men she'd taken into her bed.

"Maybe later," Hall replied.

The rider passed. He was keeping his head down as well, making it difficult for Hall to get a straight look at him until the last moment before the dark horse carried him away. When he finally did get the glimpse he'd been after, it didn't show him the sight he wanted. Hall cussed under his breath which was followed by the touch of a soft hand upon his shoulder.

"My offer still stands," the redhead told him.

Hall turned around to find the soiled dove right where he'd left her. She wore her hair in a loose braid that matched the rumpled clothes she wore. Her curves were ample and smooth and her smile came easy.

"Come on inside," she said with a wink. "Cassandra will make you feel all better."

At first, Hall intended on turning her down in a way that would leave no room for a third attempt to get him inside. After looking past her to the plush interior of the brothel, he let out a tired breath and said, "I suppose I could go for a drink."

"First one's on me." Cassandra hooked her arm around Hall's. "Once we get you off your feet, I'll see what I can do to keep you there."

Hall tightened his right arm around hers, bringing the redhead in close enough to feel the touch of her hip against him. She leaned her head on his shoulder and fell into step beside him as if she'd spent the whole month waiting on that porch for him to arrive. "You got anything special in mind?" She asked as she escorted him through the front door. "Something to drink or . . . something else?"

Hall stepped inside and looked around. The foyer was done up pretty nice, complete with burgundy rugs and a small bar serving drinks to men who sat at the little round tables scattered throughout the space. One of those men sat nursing a beer with his hat slid down toward the front of his head and one leg crossed casually over the other. When he felt a tug on his arm, Hall allowed himself to be escorted toward the bar. Along the way, he passed the man with the beer without saying a word.

"What kind of whiskey do you serve here?" he asked.

Cassandra smiled and leaned against the bar. "Anything you like, hon."

"I'll take something from the top shelf. Not the most expensive, but one or two notches down from there."

"First one's on the house," she reminded him.

"I know."

The redhead shrugged and waved to the burly man tending bar. As she ordered drinks for them both, Hall turned back around to get a look at the man with the beer. The only thing left at that table was a ring of water where his mug had been.

Hall didn't even get a chance to curse under his breath before he heard the creak of a floorboard directly beside him. Letting out a sigh, he faced the bar once again and found the man with the beer standing beside him.

"Should've let that redhead take you upstairs," he said while placing his hand upon the gun at his side. "I hear she's pretty good at what she does. Better than getting shot dead in a cathouse, that's for certain."

## Chapter Six

Hall was certain the man next to him could make good on his threat before anyone had a chance to do a damn thing about it. Rather than panic about it, however, he merely smiled and said, "If anyone would know about the talents of any given woman in any given town, it's Clint Adams."

Although he still had his hand on his Colt, Clint merely rested it there as he leaned against the bar. "I thought we got things settled between us the last time we crossed paths in Carson City. You don't follow me and I don't fill you full of lead."

"No need for the tough talk, Adams," Hall said. "I know you're not a killer."

"Then you should also remember that I don't make empty threats. Why were you following me, Jarred?"

"I wasn't sure it was you at first. Once I got a good look at your face . . ."

Cassandra sidled up to Hall and pressed against him as she leaned forward to place a glass on the bar. "Here's your whiskey," she said. "Who's your friend?"

Before Hall could answer that question, Clint said, "His friend is on his way out."

She smiled warmly when Clint tipped his hat to her and watched him carefully as he walked away from the bar and left through the front door. "I like the looks of that one," Cassandra said.

"You wouldn't be the first," Hall grunted.

"Then why don't you change my mind?" she purred. "I had my sights set on you first, you know."

After tossing back his drink, Hall said, "I know and I'm honored." He then turned toward her and asked, "What do you know about him?"

"Not much."

"Don't give me that," Hall snapped. "You watch everyone and everything in this place. Tell me what you know about that man. You can start with when he first stepped foot through that door."

"I don't like being talked to that way." When she tried to move away, Cassandra was stopped by a strong hand that clamped around her wrist. "You're hurting me."

Those three words caught the attention of a lean young man who stood in the corner of the room like a ghost. He immediately approached the bar, clenching fists that were covered in an array of cuts and scars he'd acquired in countless unpleasant encounters with unruly patrons.

Hall eased up on his grip, but didn't let her go. "Tell me what I want to know," he said.

"Or what?"

"Or you won't get the money that's in my shirt pocket." After saying that, Hall relaxed his hold on Cassandra all the way.

Pulling her hand back, she looked at Hall and then cast a quick glance at the younger man with the fists resembling ground beef. Cassandra reached into Hall's shirt pocket, found a small wad of bills and took them out. Liking what she saw, she nodded to the younger man and tucked the money between her ample breasts. "I don't know that friend of yours," she said. "First time I saw him was less than an hour before you showed up."

"Did you approach him?"

"No. I was busy."

"What about one of the other girls?" Hall asked.

"I can ask around if you like."

"Do that. I'll come back around a bit later to see what you find out."

"Is that all you'll be back for?" Cassandra asked.

Hall answered that by taking her hips in his hands, pulling her close and planting a kiss on Cassandra's lips. She was hesitant to respond at first, but quickly melted against him and slipped her tongue into his mouth. When he was through, Hall nearly had to pry her off of him so he could step away from the bar.

"Don't worry, young fella," Hall said as he passed the man with the battered fists. "You'll get another chance at me soon."

The young man was anxious to add a few fresh cuts to his fists by thumping them against Hall's face, but was held in check by the redhead, who was still reeling from her kiss.

As soon as Hall stepped outside, he took a careful look around. He didn't find a trace of Clint which came as no surprise. Adams wasn't sloppy and following hot on his heels when he'd left the cathouse would have only sparked a fight that wouldn't have been in Hall's favor. Avoiding those kinds of scuffles was one of the things that had kept Hall alive this long in the first place and he wasn't about to break from that now.

He'd found Clint before and he could do it again. When they crossed paths next time, neither of them would have the element of surprise on their side.

# Chapter Seven

*Half an hour earlier . . .*

It was getting close to midnight and Clint had scouted a good portion of the town and was satisfied nobody was shadowing his every move. Most towns would be quiet or even sleeping by now, but a place like Parker only got rowdier as the darkness got thicker and the shadows grew deeper. After finding a place to hang his hat for the night and getting a feel for the lay of the land, Clint's priority was to keep looking for Eclipse.

There were plenty of stables in town. The one that Clint had chosen to put his horses up for the night didn't have any animals for sale, but pointed him toward some that he might try. When Clint made it known that he didn't much care where the horses came from, a few more options had opened up. It was then that he'd asked about Andy Bennelli.

"Name don't sound familiar," the stableman had said. Clint only had to produce a small amount of cash from his pocket to change the filthy man's attitude. "Now I recall," he said while snatching the money from Clint's hand. "Bennelli buys and sells horses. Mostly horses that were taken from someone else."

"You mean stolen," Clint corrected.

The stableman shrugged. "Makes no difference to me."

"Where can I find Bennelli?"

"Why you looking for him?"

Nodding toward the stalls he'd rented, Clint said, "I'm looking to unload those three."

"They stolen?"

"I thought it didn't make any difference to you."

"I guess it don't."

A tense silence filled the stable as Clint felt the other man's eyes bore through him. Finally, he said, "Look, if I was the law I wouldn't need to do all this tiptoeing. I could have just arrested you and been done with it."

"True. You could have also walked in here like you did and tossed some money at me."

"I don't have all day for this," Clint said. "If you don't want to help, hand the money back to me and I'll ask someone else."

"I do wanna help," the stableman insisted. "But I also don't wanna land in jail. You gotta prove yourself if you want my help."

Clint's first instinct was to tell the stableman what he could do with whatever bit of proof he wanted and find his information somewhere else. As attractive as that was, however, time was a factor. He was certain Eclipse was somewhere in Parker, but there was no telling for how long. A horse like that would fetch a fine price and wouldn't last long in a bidding war. Also, there was always the possibility that the Darley Arabian was putting up enough of a struggle for the thief to cut his losses and . . . well . . . Clint didn't want to think about that.

"Whatever you got in mind," Clint said, "it had best be something that can be done quickly."

"Oh, it is. There's a whore working at a place down the street that robbed me blind."

"Why do I get the suspicion that you had it coming?"

"That don't matter," the stableman said through a dirty sneer. "What does matter is that she took what was in my pockets while I was passed out and didn't even touch my pecker."

"Sounds like a good night for her."

"Well not for me! Her name is Liza. She's a sweet little piece with blue eyes and a pug nose. She'll deny anything about me, so you'll need to get into her room and force her to show you where she keeps her stash."

"What stash?" Clint asked.

"Every whore's got a stash. Money, bits of jewelry, whatever she holds dear."

"What are you looking for?"

"A pocket watch that belonged to my grandpappy."

"How sentimental," Clint said.

The stableman spat on the ground and scratched his crotch. "I was gonna sell it."

"Then let me give you the money for it and we can get on with this!"

"That won't give me my proof," the other man said. "And it won't give me the joy of seein' the look on my grandmammy's face when I sell the watch back to her for a better profit I could get from any store."

There were other ways to get the information he wanted. There were other people in town who might have that information. If he found one so easily, Clint could find another. And if it was any other horse except Eclipse, he might have considered putting this slimy bastard behind him. But it was Eclipse and Clint wasn't about to cut corners after all of the hell that stallion had carried him through.

"If I do this," Clint said, "you'd better be able to tell me what I want to know."

"I've dealt with Andy Bennelli plenty of times."

"You know where I can find him?"

"Better than that, I can have him come here. All I need to do is send word that I got some healthy horses just come in and you'll get your meeting lickety split."

Since his head was spinning in trying to figure out how he'd gotten himself into this tangled mess, Clint said, "Just tell me where to find this Liza."

# Chapter Eight

There wasn't a sign posted outside the cathouse, but Clint was told the place was called The Green Rose. Finding it wasn't a problem thanks to the directions he'd been given. Finding Liza was no problem whatsoever. Any man with a pulse could have found Liza with his eyes closed and one arm tied behind his back. In fact, some men might have paid extra to find her that way.

When he got to the place, Clint went straight to the bar and was about to ask for Liza. Then he caught sight of her in the next room. She was a slender blonde with her hair cut just short enough to curl at the ends and brush her shoulders whenever she turned her head. Those shoulders were bare thanks to the dress she wore which also held her pert breasts up for all to see. She had the smooth skin and deep red lips of a girl who would carry her youth longer than most. It didn't take long for her to spot Clint. It also helped that he'd been staring at her for the last couple of seconds without blinking.

Sensing an easy mark, Liza made her way over to Clint and flashed him an even wider smile. "I haven't seen you around here, have I?"

"I just got into town," Clint replied.

"And you came right here? Must have been a long ride, cowboy."

"I'm not exactly a cowboy."

Her hand drifted down to touch Clint's modified Colt. "I can tell. You look like a man who knows how to use his gun." From there, she let her hand drift to other more interesting places below Clint's waist.

"Do you know a man named . . ."

Liza raised her eyebrows expectantly. "Yes? Named what?"

Clint's breath had been taken away by the probing little fingers sliding between his legs to tease him in spots that made him twitch. "Harry," he said as though he was spitting the word out. "Harry Brock."

She took her hand away from him while letting out a frustrated breath. "That smelly troll? What does he want?"

"He thinks you've got a watch that belongs to his grandfather."

"I've got his watch," she replied. "It belongs to me now. After what he tried to do to me, he's lucky that's all he lost."

Clint didn't ask for any details because he didn't need them and, more importantly, didn't want them. "Look, all I need is for you to . . . duck!"

Liza was confused, but before she was able to say another word, Clint slapped a hand on top of her head and pushed her down. His other hand was balled into a fist and driven into the face of a man who'd rushed up behind Liza. Knuckles met jaw in a solid crunch to send a spray of blood across the liquor bottles lined up on a shelf behind the bar.

When Clint had seen the other man coming, he'd reacted out of pure instinct. A knife was in the man's hand and the blade was on its way to Liza's back. The punch he'd delivered landed square, but it wasn't enough to put the attacker down.

Having been derailed on his first attempt, the man with the knife quickly shifted his wrath to Clint. "Step aside!" he roared.

From the corners of his eyes, Clint could see one burly young man closing in on the fellow with the knife and another smaller guy cutting through the crowd to get to the bar. Before either of those two could arrive to give the wild man the worst night of his life, Clint threw himself at the blade-wielding attacker.

The man bared his teeth and swung the knife wildly. As soon as he'd put himself between the blade and Liza, Clint raised both arms above his head and leaned back to allow the knife to pass in front of him. It came so close to opening his chest that he could feel a breeze against his shirt as the weapon sliced along its deadly course. Before the other man could take another swing at him, Clint dropped both fists like hammers. One caught the attacker's elbow, bending that arm at an awkward angle.

Snarling a guttural obscenity, the man with the knife winced in pain. Clint's other fist connected with a spot between the base of his neck and his shoulder, making the attacker's legs wobbly beneath him. Clint followed up by grabbing the other man's collar and pulling him down while bringing his knee straight up.

The man with the blade in his hand grunted something, but couldn't get a word out before his jaw was pounded by the knee that snapped his head back. Clint brought the scuffle to an end by plucking the knife from the other man's hand and driving a swift right cross into his face that sent him to the floor.

For a moment, everyone in the cathouse had their eyes glued to Clint and the man twitching near his feet. Then, as if the floorshow they'd been watching had come to an abrupt end, they went right back to their business.

One of the young men who'd meant to take care of the guy stepped forward to take the knife away. Clint handed it over, looked to Liza and tapped the groaning attacker while asking, "Do you know this gentleman?"

Her eyes were wide and her breath came in powerful bursts. Instead of answering his question, she took his face in her hands and planted a kiss on his lips that damn near made him forget he'd asked it.

## Chapter Nine

Before he knew it, Clint was being dragged into one of the little rooms upstairs. There had been some stairs and a hallway along the way, but he missed most of that due to the constant affections being lavished on him by the overly grateful blonde. When they got to the door of the little room, Liza practically used Clint as a battering ram to get it open.

"You . . . umm . . . never answered my question," Clint said in the scant seconds when his lips were free.

"Don't know him," Liza said while shoving him into her room and kicking the door shut behind her. "Probably sent by Harry."

"Does Harry have men working for him?"

"No. He threatened to hire some men. That's not hard to do around here. Now get that shirt off before I rip it off of you."

Clint tried to resist, but found it was easier to just unbutton his shirt so she would stop fussing with it. "Before we . . . hey! What are you doing now?"

Liza had already unbuckled Clint's belt and was peeling off his jeans. "What do you think I'm doing? I'm thanking you for stepping in when that mad dog tried to cut me."

"No need for all of that. I just wanted to . . ."

"Then I'm doing it because I want to. By the looks of it," she added while grasping his rigid cock, "you want it too."

"Aww, hell," Clint sighed. There would always be time for talk later. Once his shorts was off, Clint reached for Liza's blouse. He meant to unbutton it, but she shifted when he wasn't expecting it and he wound up pulling several of the buttons clean off. As they pattered against the floorboards, she looked at him with a surprised and hungry look in her eyes.

"That's more like it," she said. Liza pressed herself against him, moving her hands along his chest, back, face, or any other part of him she could reach. While her hands moved erratically, her mouth had a purpose of its own. She started by kissing him aggressively and then worked her way down to his neck. Instead of kissing, she began nibbling at his skin and then licking her way down his chest. As she went further, Liza lowered herself to her knees and wrapped her lips around Clint's erect penis.

Her frenzied efforts overpowered Clint's senses. Rather than try to direct her, he closed his eyes and sifted his fingers through her hair as she worked on him. Her lips gripped his shaft tightly and when she bobbed her head back and forth, she swirled her tongue around the tip of his cock. Suddenly, Clint was overpowered by something else. The desire he felt for her was a hunger that he had no intention of reining in.

Placing his hands on her face, he coaxed Liza to her feet. Normally, he would have picked her up and put her on the bed, but she wasn't like most women. Instead, he shoved her roughly back until she fell onto the little bed. Liza hit the mattress with a little grunt and watched him expectantly for what he would do next. Clint didn't disappoint her. He grabbed her legs, spread them apart and moved his hands up along her hips to gather her skirts up around her waist.

"Yes," she moaned. Her eyes widened further and she gripped the blankets tightly when she felt Clint's tongue trace a line along the inside of her thighs. Liza arched her back and spread her legs even wider so he could lick her wet pussy until her entire body began to tremble.

Soon, Clint stood up and positioned himself between her legs. He guided his rigid cock into her and drove all the way in with one powerful thrust. Liza let out a shuddering gasp, climaxing the moment she'd taken every inch of him inside of her. He stayed still for a short while, allowing her to regain her composure somewhat. "It's good to see you speechless for a change," he said.

Liza started to say something, but only got a few trembling gasps out before Clint was moving again. This time, he pumped in and out of her in a building rhythm. He started slow at first, but soon pounded harder and faster. Liza's pussy was dripping wet and she grunted in pleasure each time he pounded into her. When she wrapped her legs around him, Clint grabbed her hips in both hands and fucked her harder.

"Yeah," she moaned. "Just like that. Harder!"

Clint could feel another climax welling up inside of her. When it came, her entire body trembled and she pulled the blankets away from the bed. Holding her in place with both hands, Clint kept thrusting until his own pleasure built to its apex. He exploded inside of her after impaling her one last time.

He stood there, still holding Liza's legs, and noticed a small box sitting on a nearby table. Inside of it were trinkets of all kinds ranging from cigarette cases all the way down to watch fobs. While they had all most likely been taken from men's pockets, it was doubtful they'd come from the same man.

"I almost forgot," Clint said as he released her legs. "Are you attached to that watch of Harry's?"

Liza curled into a ball and nestled into the rumpled bedding. "Take it," she said breathlessly. "You earned it."

"Earned it, huh?"

"If I was already asleep and scratching myself, you'd know exactly how I felt when one of you men got through getting what you wanted."

Clint didn't have to look very long to find what he was after. The stableman had described that watch in such detail that it practically jumped out at him when he pushed aside a billfold and some loose coins.

"If you're lumping me in with every other man that's been in this room," Clint said, "then I didn't do something right."

"You did plenty right and if there's anything I can do for you, just name it."

"Actually, have you ever heard of someone named Andy Bennelli?"

Liza grinned. "Maybe."

"What have you heard?"

"The lady who runs this place has mentioned that name once or twice. I'll ask her if you like."

"I'd like that very much," Clint said. "I'll just run Harry's watch back to him and be back before you know it."

"Just wait in the bar," Liza said. "After business is done down there, we can do some more business up here."

"Now that's the kind of business I like."

Clint left the cathouse, his record of never having paid a whore still intact.

# Chapter Ten

*A short while later . . .*

Not long ago, Liza had told Clint to meet her back at the bar inside the cathouse where she worked. He'd gone back for that meeting and wasn't surprised to find that she wasn't available. Liza had a long list of regulars which was even less of a surprise. What did shock Clint was spotting Jarred Hall being led into that same cathouse by a working girl named Cassandra.

Hall was a bounty hunter who was one of the few in his profession that wasn't a hair's breadth away from being worse than the scum he dragged in for a living. He did have a wicked streak, however, and a nose for tracking that would put a hound to shame. Any bounty hunter that didn't share those characteristics wouldn't last very long in his profession.

He'd met Hall before in Carson City. It was an incident that could have gone a lot worse for both of them if they hadn't decided to help each other at the last moment. In the end, the two of them had helped put some bad men into the ground and agreed to stay out of each other's way in the future. It wound up amicable enough, but neither of them was anxious to meet the other again. Bounty hunters were inherently suspicious of their fellow man and Clint had too many enemies that were willing to pay to see him dead.

When Clint spotted Hall in the cathouse, he'd been surprised. When he'd seen the look in the bounty hunter's eyes, Clint knew it wasn't just a happy coincidence that he'd crossed paths with him again. Hall was there on business and when he'd spotted Clint, he didn't look like he was going to buy a round of beers. What seemed like even less of a coincidence was the fact that Hall showed up at the same time that Clint found himself in a hunt of his own. There were too many unknowns surrounding the theft of Eclipse, so Clint decided to bring a few things into the light.

The first step in doing that was to let Hall know he'd been spotted as well by approaching him at the bar. Clint gave him a friendly warning and left the cathouse, fully expecting to be followed on his way out. Hall wasn't hot on his trail, so Clint found a good spot to watch the cathouse from a distance. He stood in an alcove where two weather-beaten buildings leaned against each other and waited.

After a while, Hall emerged from the cathouse and looked around. Clint thought he might have been spotted but knew better when Hall bared his teeth in a quick snarl and silently grumbled to himself. Although Clint wasn't close enough to hear what the bounty hunter said, he could tell it wasn't something that should be repeated in mixed company.

Hall went back inside and stayed there. Clint got suspicious when the bounty hunter didn't show up on the street again for several minutes. Even though there were plenty of distractions inside that place, Hall wasn't the sort of man who was steered away from his chosen path very easily. Clint shifted his focus away from the cathouse, assuming that the bounty hunter had been able to slip away from there without being seen.

Knowing a fair amount about tracking from his own experience, Clint knew that any hunter's skill was put to the test when his trail inevitably went cold. It happened to the best of them and in that event, the tracker could either tirelessly search for a spot to pick up the trail again or he could take a leap. That leap had nothing to do with faith. It was guided by how well a man knew his craft and, more importantly, his prey.

Keeping to the shadows, Clint moved along the side of the street. It was the dead of night, which meant the seedy district of town was alive and kicking. There was a fair amount of people making their way to and from the opium dens and saloons. As his feet kept him moving at a steady pace, Clint's mind raced to narrow down the possibilities of what Hall would have done after going back inside that cathouse.

Surely there were at least one or two other doors out of that building. Any cathouse worth its reputation had multiple entrances to accommodate guests who didn't want to be seen coming in off the street.

If Hall had gotten this close to Clint in Parker, there was a fairly good chance that he'd been following him for some time before Clint had gotten to town. If that was the case, the bounty hunter could very well be making his way to the stable where Clint had put up those three horses for the night.

But the most likely of any possibility was that Hall was doing the same thing that Clint was doing at that moment: trying to outthink his quarry. Clint could have continued running circles in his mind to try and come up with one course after another in a desperate attempt to get one step ahead of Jarred Hall. Or, he could do one thing that wouldn't occur to most men.

It was something that had to do with any man's confidence in himself at being at the top of the pecking order. Every man had pride, but it took a finely honed instinct to know when to set that aside and admit to himself when he wasn't ahead in the game.

Clint Adams had many talents and had worn many hats. Jarred Hall, on the other hand, was a bounty hunter through and through. Clint would have bet a mighty large sum that Hall had been born a hunter and would die as one too. When facing a man like that on his playing field, there was no shame in admitting when he may very well be one step behind.

All of this flowed through Clint's mind in a rush and when he arrived at his conclusion, there was nothing for him to do other than commit to it. Clint kept his head down and his feet moving at the same pace he'd maintained since he'd first blended in with the rest of the people out scrounging for their nightly vices. Now that he'd put some distance between him and the cathouse, Clint turned toward the first alley he could find. The instant he'd taken a few steps off the boardwalk, he pivoted around to look directly behind him.

Sure enough, Hall was good enough at his job to have gotten behind Clint to follow him this far. He seemed more than a little surprised when Clint said, "You don't seem to pay much attention when I talk to you, Jarred. I believe I mentioned something about not following me."

# Chapter Eleven

Hall froze in his tracks. He'd been surprised by Clint's sudden move and his hand had reflexively gone for the Remington pistol kept in the cross-draw holster slung between his hip and belly. He was able to set aside some of his pride as well by conceding what a bad idea it would have been to clear leather. It seemed he knew his prey well enough to be certain he couldn't win in a straight contest of speed with a shooting iron.

"All right," Hall said calmly. "Now what?"

"Now," Clint replied, "you tell me what the hell you're doing."

"I'm hoping like hell you don't have business with Andy Bennelli."

"What if I do?"

"Then we've got ourselves a problem," Hall said evenly. "But I don't think that's the case. Not this time, anyway."

"Why are you here, Jarred? I know you're not hunting me."

"Yeah?"

"That's right," Clint said as he moved his hand well away from the gun at his side. "If you were, you wouldn't have been so surprised to see me back in that cathouse. Besides, I don't have a price on my head."

Jarred moved his hand away from his gun also. The smile that drifted onto his face was genuine enough when he said, "And I shouldn't have been surprised in the slightest to find Clint Adams in the midst of so many ladies."

"I don't pay for a woman's company," Clint reminded him.

"And I'm also sure you just left all those beautiful little doves alone so you could conduct yourself like a gentleman."

"I wouldn't go that far. How about you buy me a drink? I believe you owe me a few from the last time we met."

The grin that crept onto Hall's face twisted the scars on his skin into a mess of different shapes. "You talking about Carson City? That was just a whole lot of fuss over nothing, as I recall."

"You fired a few shots at me," Clint said.

"It was a misunderstanding! Kind of like what we have here."

"Which is why you owe me the drinks."

"Then you're remembering wrong, Adams. I believe you owe me a whole bottle, but I'll settle for a drink of whiskey."

"Fair enough. I know just the place."

# Chapter Twelve

The place Clint chose was a saloon that had caught his eye when he'd first ridden through town. It was located on the periphery of a busier district, affording a good view of that part of town without being enveloped by it. If there was any trouble on its way, he would most likely see it from there before it got to him. Also, there was a stack of empty beer kegs outside the saloon's front door. Any place that sold that much beer couldn't be all bad.

As soon as they'd found a place to sit and had some drinks in front of them, both men were in better spirits. "So," Clint said, "what brings you to this lovely town?"

"There's been several groups of horse thieves causing a stir through the entire state. I don't have to tell you how well that goes over in Texas."

"I think most Texans would rather lose a blood relative than a good horse."

Raising his glass, Hall said, "There's always more family. Good horses are damn rare."

Clint couldn't help but laugh at that. "Spoken like a man from a big family."

"Too big. Some of the ranchers, oil barons and other assorted rich folk around here must have had some of their stock thinned out because they pooled some resources and put a collective reward out for horse thieves."

"Collective?"

Hall grinned like a preacher discussing his favorite hymn. "Open season on all horse thieves. They're not picky about any in particular and they'll pay top dollar for any that are brought in. These men are serious, Clint. They want a clean sweep through all of Texas and they're not picky about who comes to collect."

"Sounds like things could get awfully sticky."

"Only if you've stolen a horse. So far, the contracts have all been paid and there has been plenty of thieves to go around. Once the selection starts to thin out, there's bound to be some disputes but I plan on moving on before that happens."

Clint nodded. "One thing I can vouch for is the abundance of horse thieves around here."

After thinking about that for a moment, Hall drew in a sharp breath. "Not that Darley Arabian!"

Clint nodded again.

"That explains why you're wound so tight," Hall said. "When did he go missing?"

"A day ago. I was jumped while I was sleeping out on the trail. Three of them tried to get the jump on me, but didn't get close enough to do any damage. I brought them down and that's when I saw Eclipse was already gone. Sneaky bastard came in and took him right out from under my nose."

Now it was Hall's turn to nod.

"Why are you looking so smug?" Clint asked.

"Because this sounds familiar."

"You've heard of other horses getting stolen this way?"

"Most definitely," the bounty hunter replied. "There's a small group of men that have been pulling that trick. Sending in a few decoys while the main man slithers in and out with the prize."

"If these men were decoys, they were pretty damn committed to their boss."

"That's the thing. They don't know they're decoys." Leaning forward, Hall propped his elbows on the table and lowered his voice a bit. "There's been a call for more than just bounty hunters lately. Someone's been hiring outlaws and turning them loose to raise hell. And not just in Texas either, but in Arizona and Utah as well."

"Why?"

Hall shrugged. "I don't give a damn. When some rich man decides to put a price on that information, then I'll look into why. Until then, I'll keep doing what I do best and stash my money away. So as far as your problem is concerned, I take it you tracked your horse here?"

"Yeah," Clint said. "I've heard he's supposed to be sold to some outlaw piece of trash named Andy Bennelli."

"That's no surprise. Bennelli buys and sells plenty of stolen animals in these parts. If he doesn't make the deal, he probably arranged it. Where'd you come by that information?"

"From one of the men who raided my camp. One of the decoys you mentioned."

"And you got him to talk?" Hall mused. "Good work. Did he tell you much before you killed him?"

"I didn't kill him."

"Then you handed him over to the law." Shaking his head, the bounty hunter added, "Probably didn't even ask about a reward, either. Bloody amateurs running around ruining things for us professionals."

Since Hall was obviously trying to get under Clint's skin by calling him an amateur, Clint didn't react to the slight. Instead, he took some pleasure in saying, "He's still with me. Now that I know about the reward straight from a professional of your caliber, maybe I will turn him in. Thanks for parting with that information, by the way."

Hall glanced to his left and right. "I don't see anyone with you. Didn't see anyone with you back at the cathouse, either."

"He's been wrapped up good and tight ever since I found him at my camp. I brought him along in case there were any other questions I needed answered."

"Clint Adams taking prisoners?"

"He's tied to a chair in my hotel room," Clint chuckled. "Not exactly what I'd call a prisoner."

"Did he happen to tell you who managed to steal your horse?"

"He did."

Hall chuckled and took another drink. "Cagey as always, Adams. What's the matter? You don't trust me?"

"Occupational hazard."

"What occupation are you in these days?"

"My occupation doesn't hold the hazard of being seen as untrustworthy," Clint said. "Yours does."

"That's some mighty righteous talk coming from a man like you," Hall said.

"And just what the hell does that mean?"

"It means when I wanted to track you down, all I had to do was listen for the sound of a woman's grunting and groaning. And even when I'm not looking for you, there you are . . . dipping your wick like always."

Clint drank his beer and replied, "Don't be jealous just because some men can get the job done where a lady is concerned. What the hell were you doing in that cathouse anyway? Since you're obviously so pious, I would've thought you wouldn't want to go anywhere near those wicked women."

"I was told that one of the men high up on that collective list I mentioned would be in this vicinity."

"And?"

"He wasn't."

Clint's mug was empty, so he swirled some of the remaining suds at the bottom. "You think he spotted you?"

"I doubt it."

"All right then," Clint said. "I'll stop being cagey. Victor Howlett."

Hall furrowed his brow. "What's that name mean to you?"

"That's the man who stole Eclipse. That's the man I've been tracking and something tells me you've got a connection to him as well."

"You could always read a man like a book. If I recall, that made you a real devil at the poker table."

"Devil enough to clean you out," Clint said.

"Fair enough. So did you happen to find Howlett?"

"Why do you ask? Looking to snag him for yourself?"

"Would it matter if I was?" Hall asked. "After all, you're interested more in justice than any sort of reward. Am I right?"

"Funny how when you say the word justice, it rings as true as an atheist quoting the bible."

Rather than debate on just how close to the mark Clint's barbed comments might have hit, Hall said, "My point is that if I was looking to get him for myself, we both know I could find him no matter who else was looking or trying to protect him. If I wasn't before, then I sure as hell am now. You may not be a bounty hunter, but you've got to have a notion of how much someone would be willing to pay to catch a thief good enough to get one over on someone like you."

"Enough with the flattery," Clint groaned. "It doesn't suit you. Why don't we just strike a bargain? Since we're both after the same people, let's work together. I get Eclipse and you get to take these fools off my hands when we're through."

"Halfway partners! Reminds me of Carson City."

"Christ almighty, let's hope not."

# Chapter Thirteen

Clint strode into the stable, feeling every second of the last twenty-four hours weighing on his back. He'd had worse days, but it had almost been that long since he'd gotten a chance to get more than a few winks of sleep. Once he reminded himself of what he was after, he woke up quicker than if a bucket of cold water had been thrown into his face.

"You find my watch?" the stableman asked.

Reaching into his pocket, Clint removed the timepiece he'd acquired from Liza and held it in front of him. "It's right here. What's the matter, Harry? You look surprised to see me again."

"It's just . . . uhh . . . give it here!"

Clint pulled the watch away half a second before it was snatched from him. "Not so fast. We had a deal, remember? Tell me where to find Andy Bennelli."

"Give me the watch first."

"Fine." Clint handed it to the stableman. "Now, where do I find Bennelli?"

"Up yer ass!" Harry replied through a leering smile.

A few seconds ticked by. In those moments, the only sounds within the stable were the rustling of hooves and

Harry's excited breathing. After a few more seconds passed, that breathing became a little less anxious.

Just then, a side door was knocked open by a short, dirty-faced man who'd used his forehead as a battering ram. Hall was behind him holding his Remington to the back of the smaller man's head. Using the barrel of his pistol to move the other man along, Hall said, "I think that was supposed to be this one's cue."

"You didn't look too good before, Harry," Clint said. "Now it seems like you might get sick."

"No," Harry sputtered. "I don't know who that is."

"In that case, I guess I can go ahead and shoot him," Hall said as he thumbed back the hammer of his Remington.

"God damn it, Harry!" the dirty-faced man said in a rush. "You said this'd be easy money!"

"What's going on between you and Bennelli?" Clint asked. "You two blood related? Must be something pretty special for you to want to protect him like this."

"I just . . . it's just that I didn't think you'd hold up your end," Harry said.

"Right. Especially since you already hired some other men to go after that damn watch. All I'm looking for is a nod in the right direction. Point me toward Bennelli and we're through."

"There's a dry goods store on the east end of town, right next to—"

"A hat shop?" Clint asked.

"Yeah! That's the place! That's where Bennelli does his business. Leastways, that's where I send folks looking to buy or sell stolen horses. That's all I know. I swear to Christ."

Clint shook his head in disgust. He was about to walk away when he had to stop and ask, "Why was that such a chore?"

"Huh?"

"All this fussing about with a damn pocket watch, setting up this half-assed ambush, trying to talk tough. What the hell was the reason for any of it?"

Harry's shoulders drooped and his head hung low. "This watch really did belong to my grandpappy," he said.

Clint balled up his fist and was set to knock Harry onto his ass when he decided it wouldn't be worth the ache he'd feel in his knuckles afterward. "Let's go," he snarled.

But Hall wasn't quick to put an end to it so quickly. "Aren't those horses yours?" he asked.

Clint glanced toward the stables and nodded. "They belonged to the men who attacked my camp, so I suppose they belong to me now."

"Then why don't we sell them to Bennelli?"

"You can get a good price," Harry said out of reflex. "Especially if'n I put a good word in for you."

"Just set it up," Hall told the stableman. "And if you try to double cross us, this man here will pay the price first and you'll pay soon after."

The dirty-faced man was the first one on that list and he said, "I'll go set up the deal." Glaring at Harry, he added, "That prick wouldn't give a damn if you shot me anyhow."

"I'll go with you," Clint said. "Jarred, stay here and keep an eye on Harry." When the stableman tried to assert himself, Clint put him in his place with a swift punch to the jaw. It wasn't enough to knock the stableman out, but it did a fine job of shutting Harry up for a spell.

Hall holstered his Remington and allowed his former hostage to walk toward the stable's main door. "Don't make me chase you!" he said. And, like a dog on a leash, the smaller man stayed put before getting too far away. "Why don't the two of you put the reins on them horses." Once Harry and the other man raced to do what they were told, Hall approached Clint.

"I can handle myself just fine," Clint said as the bounty hunter walked up to him. "Someone should go with him just to make sure he doesn't fly the coop."

"I know," Hall said. Once he was standing within arm's reach of Clint, he lowered his voice a bit and asked, "You want me to go? You seem kinda flustered."

"Damn right I'm flustered. Dealing with so many assholes in one day is wearing me down."

Hall gave him a slap on the back. "I know just how you feel, Adams. Your problem here is that you're looking for too many answers."

"They're what I need if I'm going to find Eclipse before it's too late."

"I'm talking about that business with the watch. Sometimes, you just need to accept the fact that men like these two are idiots. They don't always make sense and trying to figure out why they do what they do just complicates things. Let's face facts," Hall added. "If these morons had a brain in their heads, they'd be bankers or something."

After taking hold of the reins to the three horses, Clint started walking toward the front door where the smaller man was waiting. "If I'm not back in half an hour," he said while pointing at Harry, "kill him. Slowly."

The command may have been a bluff, but it was worth it to Clint just to see the color drain from Harry's face.

# Chapter Fourteen

When Clint and his new associate walked those three horses down the street, they got more than a few sideways glances. Obviously, the dirty-faced man was known in Parker and he wasn't too happy about being seen under the thumb of someone else.

"What's your name, anyway?" Clint asked.

"Ed."

"Seems like you've got a lot of friends around here, Ed. You're a lucky man."

Looking at a pair of rough fellows wearing two guns apiece, Ed cringed as both of those men pointed and laughed at him. "Yeah. Real lucky."

"What do they think is so funny?"

"I just struck out to work for myself three days ago. Told these assholes I wasn't about to let anyone lead me around by the nose anymore."

"That's a real shame, Ed. Maybe you should get into another line of work. Like banking, perhaps."

Since he hadn't been privy to Clint's conversation with Hall, Ed didn't find that comment to be very amusing. Clint chuckled anyway and gave Ed a shove. The fact remained that some men were born good and some were born bad. Others were just born to be filthy little rats who got pushed around by stronger men. In his youth, Clint might have felt sorry for those in the last category. After spending enough time seeing just how cruel the world was, he'd learned that more often than not, those rats got what they deserved.

The streets became much less crowded once they put the entertainment district behind them. It was a short walk to the dry goods store and Clint got there without wasting any time. Even so, there were three men emerging from the place as he and Ed approached it. They didn't seem to be expecting them, but they weren't exactly about to welcome them either.

"What the hell you lookin' at?" one of the men snapped. He was a tall fellow with long, stringy hair and a bowler hat.

"There a law against taking a walk in this town?" Clint replied.

"If you're out for a walk, then keep walking!" Grinning, the tall man added, "You licking this one's boots now, Ed? I thought you were gonna go into business for yourself."

Ed kept his mouth shut.

The three men chuckled at Ed's expense, but got serious again when it became clear that Clint wasn't going to be cowed so easily. Standing next to the tall one was a Mexican with a scalp that had been shorn almost down to the skin and a squat man carrying a shotgun. All three stared at Clint as if Ed meant less than nothing.

"You deaf, mister?" the tall man growled. "I told you to move along."

"I'm looking for Andy Bennelli," Clint said.

"What for?"

"I've got some horses to sell."

"We don't know you," the Mexican replied. "Sell your animals somewhere else."

"You know me," Ed said.

When Clint heard Ed's voice, his first instinct was to react as though he'd been thrown to the wolves. But it seemed that Ed wasn't trying to cause any trouble just yet so Clint waited to see where he was headed.

"You're a messenger," said the tall man.

"And I'm bringing you a message. This man has three horses to sell."

"Just take me to Andy Bennelli," Clint said. "We'll straighten everything out."

The front door of the dry goods store was opened by a man who was easily a foot shorter than almost everyone else in the vicinity. He had a solid, muscular build and hair that stood out at wild angles that made him look like more of an animal than a man. He took one step outside, surveyed what was happening with dark eyes and immediately drew his pistol. Locking a glare onto Clint, he said, "Kill those sons of bitches!"

## Chapter Fifteen

All three of the other men in front of the store reacted instantly. The man with the shotgun brought the weapon up to fire while the other two went for the pistols at their sides. Despite being surprised by how quickly the fight had started, Clint wasn't about to be cut down in the street by the likes of them.

Without taking his eyes from his targets, Clint drew the Colt from its holster and dropped to one knee. Since the scattergun was the one that needed the least amount of skill to be put to deadly use, he sent his first round at the man carrying it. His round burned a hole through the shotgunner's chest, knocking him back so he emptied his barrels amid a clap of thunder that sent a whole lot of buckshot into the sky.

The short man who'd gotten this ball rolling stayed in the doorway of the store which also put him behind the row of three men in front of the place. He fired a shot at the easiest target, which was Ed. After putting a bullet straight through Ed's heart, he ducked back inside and fired once more at the street to cover his departure.

"Don!" The Mexican hollered. "Get out here!" The Mexican had his pistol in hand and was sighting along the top of its barrel when Clint's attention was shifted in his direction. The modified Colt barked once more, spitting a round that punched through the Mexican's skull. As the Mexican dropped, another man filled the doorway of the dry goods store.

The tall gunman was the first one to fire back at Clint. He did so in a series of fast pulls of his trigger that sent lead hissing through the air to Clint's left. His shots may have been wild, but they were drawing closer so Clint answered back with a shot of his own. That one clipped the tall man in the shoulder without doing much damage.

"Clear a path!" the man in the doorway, who Clint guessed was Don, said. Without waiting for anyone to react to his request, Don fired at the street. Since he pulled his trigger without taking a moment to aim, the street was the only thing he had any chance of hitting.

Clint had used half of the rounds in his Colt. Rather than waste another, he shifted the odds more into his favor by making a move that none of the gunmen expected. He rushed straight at the tall man. Not only did that rattle the biggest gunman, but it also put him between Clint and the others who were trying to gun him down. He reached the tall man after three bounding strides, deciding that he would knock the guy down unless he was forced into something more drastic. The tall man sealed his fate by bringing his pistol around to fire another wild shot that whipped through the air several feet over Clint's head. Instead of waiting for the big man's aim to improve, Clint put him down with a single bullet through the heart.

Apart from Don, there was another weapon being fired from the dry goods store. Clint recognized the cracking shots as coming from a Sharps rifle. The rifle's barrel was hard to miss. It protruded from a broken window of the store with smoke still curling from its tip. Now that he was already much closer to the storefront, Clint leaped onto the boardwalk in front of the place and grabbed the barrel of the Sharps.

The iron was still hot from the rounds that had been fired, but that didn't stop Clint from tightening his grip and pulling the rifle through the window. His intention had been to take the weapon away, but he received a bonus when the man behind the rifle decided not to let go of his weapon. The expression on his face was priceless since he seemed just as surprised to be yanked from the store as Clint was to see him flop through the window. To make things even better, the man cracked his head on the wooden frame of the window that had been raised to allow him to poke his nose outside. His head snapped back with a sickening thump and it was plain to see that he was knocked cold, leaving Clint with the Sharps rifle in hand.

When he saw movement from the doorway, Clint pointed both his Colt and the newly acquired Sharps at the man who'd stepped outside. "Stay right where you are!" he yelled.

Don stood rooted to his spot.

"Where's Andy Bennelli?" Clint snarled.

"G-gone."

"What about the short, scraggly fella?"

"He's gone too."

"Don't play with me!" Clint roared as he made his way to the front door. "That short fella was just here!"

"And he just left," Don replied in a rush. "Him and Andy both."

The inside of the dry goods store was exactly what anyone would have expected. It was mostly open space with several long tables and a few shelves along the walls, all of which was laden with various bits of merchandise. Don stood near the door, bumping against a counter where the cash register was kept.

"Where'd they go?" Clint asked.

"Out back. They went . . ."

Clint holstered his Colt so he could hold the Sharps properly. Prodding Don with the rifle barrel, he said, "Drop the gun!"

Don did as he was told, although he was so flustered that he seemed to have forgotten he was even holding a pistol.

"Now show me where they went," Clint demanded.

"They went out back."

"Lead the way and do it fast."

Although Don shuffled his feet at first, a few knocks from Clint was more than enough to get him moving. He took Clint straight to the shop's back door, which Clint shoved him through in case anyone was waiting to spring an ambush out there. Nobody fired a shot, so Clint came outside as well.

Without any torches or light of any kind out there, Clint could barely make out a mix of several large shapes moving away from the lot behind the store. The rumble of horses' hooves was unmistakable.

Clint called out to Eclipse, but heard no change in the pounding of the hooves. Other than that, he thought he heard wagon wheels and some men's voices. All of those sounds quickly faded as the whole group rode further into the darkness.

# Chapter Sixteen

"Stay put!" Clint snarled as he turned and stormed through the store. He went straight to the front door, climbed onto one of the horses he'd brought and rode the animal bareback around the building.

Even though his eyes were adjusted to the dark, there was precious little to see. The sounds he'd heard were gone and when he tried to ride in the direction they'd last been, he quickly came up against a few more buildings that practically leapt out at him from the thick shadows. Just riding that short distance was enough for him to realize the sounds he was hearing could be coming from anywhere for miles ahead of him. Worse than that, those sounds were blending in with the rest of the noise coming from the rowdier sections of Parker.

"God damn it!" Clint said as he turned the horse around and returned to the dry goods store. To his surprise, Don was still where he'd left him.

When he saw the expression on Clint's face, Don shrugged and said, "You told me to stay put."

"Where did they go?" Clint asked while dropping down from the horse's back.

"Probably the same place they always go when they get some horses that're worth keeping."

"And where's that?"

"West."

Clint grabbed hold of Don by the collar. "Don't make me drag it out of you," he warned. "I'm not in the mood for a long conversation."

Don held his hands up as if he had any chance of warding Clint away. "I don't know a lot more than that. Usually, the horses are just sold off, but every so often, they take some West. Since they're not usually back in less than a few days, they must be going into New Mexico. If they were headed any further than that, they'd be gone longer."

"How often do they make those runs across the border?"

"Usually once a month. They just got a fine stallion in and were gonna head out anyway."

"Until they got spooked."

Don shook his head. "I think it was a coincidence. Could have been they knew someone might be coming for that stallion, but I doubt it. They were set to make that ride either today or tomorrow."

"If they weren't spooked, then you're telling me they would normally ride out in the middle of the night?" Clint said.

"Yeah. They would. They all know the way with their eyes closed and Victor's got eyes like a hawk. I swear to the Lord that man can see in the dark. Some say he just knows this part of the country so well he can get to every little cave without having to look." Snapping out of the admiring haze he'd fallen into, Don quickly added, "Ask anyone."

"Can you take me to where they went?" Clint asked.

"Not in the dark!"

"What about at first light?"

Don winced. "I can get you a little ways in the right direction, I suppose. I've gone with them one time before. I should be able to recall a few landmarks."

"Just a few?"

"Once I get out there, some things might start to look familiar. Please," Don frantically added. "I'll do my best, just don't kill me."

It wasn't until then that Clint realized he was still hanging on to Don's shirt in a grip so tight that his knuckles had turned white. More than that, his other hand had come to rest upon his holstered Colt and was tensed as if ready to draw and fire the pistol at any second. Suddenly, it didn't seem strange that Don was being so cooperative.

Deciding to play on the fear that was already inside the other man, Clint asked, "How many others are here?"

"They're gone. Or dead."

"Who else is on the way?"

"Nobody! I swear. Please. If there is anyone coming, they'll probably just want to watch a fight. Now that the shooting's stopped, they'll just get back to what they were doing. That's how it is around here at this time of night. Any respectable folk lock themselves into their homes at sundown and stay there."

"What about the law?"

Don chuckled until he saw that Clint wasn't joining in. "I thought you were kidding about the law."

"There's no law in Parker?"

"There's a sheriff, but he's more of a street sweeper, comes along to clean up the bodies once the fights are over. He'll probably make it here after breakfast."

Clint released his grip on Don's shirt, only to drop that same hand onto the man's shoulder. "Don't worry," he said as he shoved him out the front door. "We'll be away from this pit of a town before then."

# Chapter Seventeen

"So?" Hall said when Clint returned to the stable. "Did everything go as planned?"

Clint scowled at the bounty hunter. "Not exactly. Didn't you hear the shooting?"

"There's been shooting here and there all night long. This is a wild town. I'm definitely coming back here for another visit sometime." Pointing his Remington at Harry, he added, "If this one double-crossed us, then we all know what comes next."

"I didn't double cross nobody!" Harry said. "All I did was send word to Bennelli that someone was coming with some horses to sell. I did it the same way I did it every other time!"

"Let him go," Clint said.

"You sure about that?" Hall asked.

"Things went south, but not because of him. But if he doesn't forget all about us and what happened here tonight as soon as we leave," Clint said to the trembling liveryman, "then we'll be back and we won't be happy."

Harry nodded quickly. "I'll hold up my end. No problems here, mister. None at all."

With that, Clint gathered up his saddle and headed outside with Don following him like an obedient puppy.

Hall emerged from the livery and strode a few paces to catch up with him. "Mind telling me who the hell this is?" he said while giving Don a not-so-gentle nudge.

As he led the way down the street a ways, Clint found a hitching post without anyone nearby and tied the horses off. He then told Hall what had happened at the dry goods store while placing his saddle on the horse he'd chosen for the ride into town.

"So what do you intend on doing with another prisoner?" Hall asked. "Or are we not taking prisoners?"

Clint hadn't thought Don could be any more nervous. He was proven wrong when he saw the sweat break out onto Don's face to cover him in a sheen that glistened in the flickering light cast by a nearby torch. "He can help us find where we need to go."

"Really?"

"That's what I said, isn't it?"

"It's just that he looks like he'll say just about anything to save his life. Actually," Hall added, "it looks like he won't be able to say much of anything at all."

As if to prove his point, Don tried to say something in his defense and only managed to sputter a few quaky syllables.

"He worked with Bennelli and knows a thing or two. He wasn't valuable enough for any of the others to save before they left, but he must have seen some things we can use."

"If he knew anything worth knowing," Hall said, "one of those outlaws would have also tried killing him rather than leaving him with us."

By the time they'd reached the hotel where Clint had rented his room, Don finally managed to steady himself enough to say, "They wouldn't do anything like that. At least . . . I don't think they would."

Ignoring the frightened man, Hall asked, "Where was this place anyway?"

"Right there," Clint replied as he pointed across the street.

Within a stone's throw of the hotel was a short row of storefronts including a hat shop and the dry goods store. There were bodies still laying outside of the place, but were easily overlooked in the inky darkness and the other pieces of trash scattered in the deeply rutted street.

"That's the place where you met up with those horse thieves?" Hall asked.

"Sure is," Clint replied.

"No wonder you knew right where to find it. At least you're getting to know this town inside and out."

"For all the good it'll do us. We're leaving."

"No, Adams. We ain't."

Clint chose to ignore those words as he hitched the horses in front of the hotel. "I'm going in to fetch my things. You want to help me with the man I got tied in there or do you just want to watch over this one?"

"I'll take this one with me and we'll all ride out in the morning," Hall said.

"Strictly speaking, it is morning," Clint said. "Very early morning. It'll be light before you know it."

"Which means we can get a bit of sleep before riding." Seeing that he was being ignored once again, Hall moved to stand in front of Clint and stop him with an outstretched hand.

Looking down at the bounty hunter's arm, Clint said, "That's a real good way to lose that."

"I know you're fond of your horse," Hall said. "Hell, I'd be riled up too if it was my horse that got stolen. But we won't do any good for any one or any horse if we go floundering around in the dark on a trail we don't know while we're too tired to see straight."

"I've been through West Texas plenty of times," Clint told him.

"Enough to know this particular stretch of trail better than men who've made it their business to ride this route come rain or shine?"

Clint didn't have an answer for that.

"In fact, we'd have to know this terrain better than those men because the bastards we're after are horse thieves. If there's anything more slippery than a horse thief in Texas, I don't know what the hell it is. Those men will know exactly where to look for anyone following them and they'll have plenty of hiding spots and ambush points in mind to deal with anyone they find." Jabbing a finger against Clint's chest, Hall added, "You know I'm right."

"Every second we waste now, those assholes get farther away from here!"

"I know."

"And I suppose that suits you just fine," Clint growled.

"It does." Before Clint could say anything else or even possibly take a swing at him, Hall added, "Because I know I can track a trout through white water and you can handle anything these fools can throw at us just so long as you're not falling out of your saddle from exhaustion."

"I'm not that tired."

"But you'll be better after some sleep and you'll be able to see more than ten feet in front of you."

Clint sighed. "So your plan is to butter me up to get your way?"

"Hell no! My plan is to track these men down. That's what I do."

"I can track them just fine on my own."

Hall spat out a single laugh. "You might be able to do some tracking but me . . . I'm magic."

# Chapter Eighteen

It was amazing what a little bit of sleep could do. When he'd first climbed into bed, Clint thought he'd wait for a short while and then strike out on his own after Eclipse and the horse thieves. As soon as his feet were up and his head was down, however, he knew that Hall had been right. Clint wound up getting just a few hours of shut-eye, but he felt like a new man when he awoke.

Sven hadn't moved very much since being tied to a chair and stuck in one corner of the room. It wasn't until that morning that Clint realized the lanky rustler had been asleep most of the time. He woke up, peeled his eyes open and looked around. "Wh . . . what happened? Am I in jail yet?"

"Not yet," Clint replied. "We've got some riding to do."

"But my leg. It's wounded."

"Stop your whining. It's barely more than a scratch."

"But it hurts!"

Wheeling around and placing his hand upon the Colt at his side, Clint asked, "You want it to hurt a lot more?"

Clint may not have been the sort of man to kick a man when he was down or tied to a chair, but Sven didn't know that. Shrinking into his seat, Sven said, "No, sir."

"Good. Now keep your mouth shut while I get everything situated."

As Clint stuffed his things into his saddlebags, Sven said, "Mind if I ask where we're headed?"

"Same as before. We're going to reclaim my horse."

"He's probably a long ways from here by now."

"I know he is," Clint said. "And you're going to help take me there."

"All I did was help steal them horses," Sven insisted. "Then I delivered them to some other fellas who took them from there. That's it!"

"I'm sure you picked up something along the way."

Sven shook his head vigorously. "If I knew anything, I'd tell you, but I don't know a damn thing. Honest!"

Now that he was done packing his saddlebags, Clint approached Sven's chair. He didn't make a move toward his gun or do anything meant as a threat to the other man. Even so, Sven looked ready to wriggle out of his own skin. "I can think of at least one thing you could tell me that would be a help," Clint said.

"Wh . . . what?"

"Where you delivered those horses after stealing them."

"That's easy. Andy Bennelli has a place in Parker. It's right next to—"

"A hat shop," Clint interrupted. "I was already there. In fact, you can see the hat shop from this window."

"Really? How'd you manage that?"

Clint shrugged. "Lucky, I guess."

"Oh. Then I suppose you don't need me."

"Where did the horses go from there?"

A fresh wave of dread washed over Sven's face. "Aw, how the hell should I know?"

"That's why you're coming with us."

"Us? You mean, more than just you?"

"That's right," Clint said cheerily. "Wouldn't want you to get lonely. By the way," he added while untying the ropes that were wrapped around Sven's torso and the back of the chair, "feel free to make as much noise as you want. There's no law around here and if anyone comes to your rescue, I imagine they're someone else I'd like to have a word with."

Sven had plenty to say after that, but he kept most of it down to barely audible grunts and mumbles as he was untied. After allowing Sven to untie his own ankles, Clint loaded him up with the saddlebags and marched him outside. Hall was waiting for him there with the horses. Don had his hands tied behind his back and was already perched on one horse's back.

"Looks like you got yourself a pack mule," the bounty hunter chided. "Maybe he should be fitted for a saddle."

"Real funny," Sven grunted. "Which of those horses is mine?"

"This beaut right here," Hall said as he patted the flank of the animal already bearing Don's weight.

"What about that one?" Sven whined as he nodded to one of the other horses. "Or that one there?"

"This is mine," Hall replied as he scratched one of the other horses behind its ear. "And we had to leave one horse with the stableman to keep him happy so he wouldn't mention us to anyone else for a while. Clint's already staked a claim on that other one."

"That leaves you with your new friend over there," Clint said. "Unless you really would rather walk?"

Sven kept on grousing to himself as he climbed onto the horse's back. Once there, he was tied up with a rope that connected him to Don before being securely knotted to the saddle horn.

"There we go," Hall said. "If one of them takes a tumble, they both do. And if they do, they'll be dragged behind this filly for a ways. They'd better be worth the effort."

"We'll find out soon enough," Clint said.

# Chapter Nineteen

Tracking any man or beast was always easier if the hunter knew exactly where to pick up the trail. In this case, all Clint and Hall had to do was go around to the back of the dry goods store to find the spot where Howlett and the rest had started the previous night's ride. It also helped that they had light to guide them, but Hall was already smug enough without Clint letting him know he'd made the right call in waiting for morning.

"Looks like they were driving a buckboard as well," Hall said.

Clint sat on his horse, keeping watch over the prisoners and anyone who might happen along. "I did hear wagon wheels when they left," he said. "They were heading West. I was told they're bound for New Mexico."

"So you said last night. Let's get going, then."

"You've already seen everything you need?" Clint asked. "But we haven't even been here for ten minutes."

"Didn't I tell you I was the best tracker in this part of the country?"

"What you said was that you're magic."

Hall smiled broadly. "And how very nice that you remembered."

"I remember plenty of things," Clint said. "Doesn't mean I believe them. I don't intend on coming back to this mud hole of a town if I can help it, so I want to make sure we get what we need the first time around."

"Hey Don, refresh Mister Adams' memory about how often horses were taken from here."

Grudgingly, the prisoner replied, "Few times a month."

"I'd wager it was more often than that," Hall said. "Either that, or they'd been running this particular route for a good long time because these here tracks are piled so high on top of one another I'm surprised they ain't made a hill just yet."

"Wouldn't it be a rut?" Sven asked.

"Either way, there's so many tracks left by the same wagon and so many horses leading in one direction that we could very well have followed them at night." Seeing the scowl on Clint's face, Hall quickly added, "That was just a joke, Adams. We can follow them just fine now, so let's get a move on."

Clint had done plenty of tracking in his time. Even on his worst day, he couldn't have missed the ones left behind by the countless times those horse thieves had headed west from that lot. Allowing Hall to take the lead,

Clint kept hold of the third horse's reins and followed the bounty hunter through town.

The tracks were easy to read along the side streets and narrow paths that cut through Parker's mercantile district. That was a fancy name for a motley assortment of feed and supply stores peppered in among a tailor and tannery. After going down an alley and joining up with one of the larger streets, the tracks led them to the edge of town and toward the trail heading to open country. The horizon stretched out in front of them, giving a clear view of West Texas and the rockier terrain beyond. Even though Clint could still see the tracks they'd been using as a guide, the task was becoming harder with every passing minute.

About four miles outside of Parker, Hall pulled back on his reins just enough to let Clint catch up to him. "You keep along this trail. I'm circling around that way."

Clint looked in the direction Hall had pointed without seeing much of anything. "Why?"

"Because that's where the tracks lead."

"Only tracks I see are from the wagon and they stick to this path."

"And that," Hall said, "is why I'm the one following these other tracks." Seeing that his smart-mouth response wasn't going over too well with its audience, Hall added, "There's a break in the trail and some tracks left behind by a pair of horses. These look fresh, but there are other older ones beneath them."

Clint leaned forward in his saddle and squinted down at the ground. Although he did see a spot where the brush and weeds just off the trail had been trampled, he didn't see enough to come to the same conclusion as Hall.

"Look," the bounty hunter said. "They're there. If you're gonna second-guess everything I do, then we might as well go our separate ways right now."

"I'm not second-guessing you. I was just looking to see those tracks you mentioned."

"You want me to climb down from my saddle and point them out to you? Maybe a free lesson in tracking to go along with it?"

"Just get moving," Clint said. "Or I can give you a free lesson in dropping a man from his saddle before he knows what hit him."

"You're an amusing man, Adams. That's why I think I'm gonna like riding with you."

"I wasn't joking about dropping you from your saddle, you know."

"I know," Hall said while riding away. "Most men are full of hot wind. You ain't. That keeps things interesting."

After Hall rode away, Don grumbled, "Amusing ain't the same as interesting."

"Shut up," Clint snapped.

# Chapter Twenty

Hall snapped his reins and kept his eyes on the ground directly in front of him. He trusted his horse well enough to let the animal worry about navigating the terrain while he concerned himself with following the tracks he'd discovered. For a man of his experience, the imprints leading away from the main trail stood out like a lump of coal on a field of snow. Considering that those tracks had been left by horse thieves on the move, it seemed most likely that at least one or two scouts had separated from the rest to look for lawmen or anything else that might get in their way.

He was confident in his assessment when the tracks led him toward some rocks and grew even more confident when those rocks formed a rise that would allow the riders to get a better look at the surrounding land. When the tracks led down the rise and even further away from the trail, he started to have some doubts. Hall wasn't about to doubt what his instinct and senses had been telling him. Instead, he doubted the conclusions he'd drawn.

Getting away from the trail and onto higher ground made perfect sense to scout ahead or take a look behind.

From there, the tracks should have circled back around to the trail or at least headed in a similar direction so the riders could catch up again in a short amount of time. But the tracks continued to move down the rise and into the rocks. If they were headed toward some sort of hiding spot or a place to hole up for a while, then the wagon should have gone as well. Not only were there no fresh wheel tracks to be found, but there weren't even any ruts to tell him that a wagon had gone that way before.

Hall slowed his pace a bit, but kept moving forward. He didn't like it when his instincts were wrong. It wouldn't be the first time such a thing happened, but whenever it did, he got a feeling at the bottom of his gut that a man got when just starting to fall after taking a wrong step at the top of a staircase. What usually followed that feeling wasn't very good. That's why a man who felt it had to prepare himself for the worst.

Reaching to his holster, Hall drew his Remington and rested it upon his knee. If someone was going to take a shot at him, they wouldn't do it without having to dodge a few bullets themselves.

The tracks he followed weren't as pronounced as the ones that had led him away from Parker. At first, he'd figured that the men who rode this way were more careful. There were certainly fewer of them than what had beaten the main path out of town. But now that he'd followed them for a while longer, Hall could tell that the horses that had gone this way had done so at a slow, plodding pace.

Soon, he caught sight of a different set of tracks overlapping the first ones. Those were sharper and cleaner. They'd been left by animals moving with purpose. They were also heading back in the opposite direction. Hall pulled back on his reins and stood in his stirrups. He could see no hint of an ambush. Apart from a general nervousness caused by the unknown, his gut wasn't telling him much of anything.

Something was up ahead. It might not have been an immediate threat to him, but it was definitely something. Hall was a thorough man, but he was also curious. Both of those reasons drove him onward with a healthy sense of caution keeping the gun in his hand.

Now it was Hall who started riding at a slower pace. When he spotted the dark opening situated between what looked like two piles of broken rocks, he climbed down from his saddle and stalked forward on foot. He kept his reins in one hand, the Remington in the other, and his eyes fixed on a point directly ahead.

Less than twenty paces later, his horse started getting anxious.

"What's the matter, girl?" Hall whispered. "If you're thinking there's something peculiar in those rocks, I'm beginning to agree with you."

Before long, Hall decided to tie his horse off and continue alone. His animal wasn't about to disagree with that decision and waited anxiously for him to return.

The path leading to that opening looked like it had once been a stream. A smooth stone bed was colored by old silt and mud that was caked on like so many layers of paint. The opening Hall had spotted at first was actually an archway formed by boulders and a couple of old tree trunks. He tightened his grip on the Remington, even though his senses gave him no reason to fret. After taking another step, a smell reached his nose that put a grimace on his face.

Hall kept walking. When he reached the arch, he stood in the shade until his eyes became accustomed to the shadows. There was a cave further back in the darkness. Now that he was closer to it, the smell became a stench that clung to his nose and wouldn't let him go. It was the stench of death and he knew it would be with him for a long time once he'd put that cave behind him.

As far as Hall was concerned, that moment couldn't come fast enough.

# Chapter Twenty-One

Clint didn't see Hall for several hours, which didn't bother him in the slightest. It did, however, make his two reluctant companions more than a little nervous.

"Where'd he go?" Don asked.

"You heard what he said just as well as I did," Clint replied. "He's scouting."

"Shouldn't he be back by now?"

"Depends on what he found."

Don let the matter rest for all of three seconds before asking, "Aren't you curious or maybe a little concerned?"

"What's the matter? Did you two form some kind of close bond during the time you spent in Parker?"

"Don't be a damn fool!" The moment those words left his mouth, Don obviously regretted them. Actually, he regretted them the moment Clint turned in his saddle to lock a harsh glare directly on him.

"What I mean," Don amended, "is that you're obviously not a fool. Something might have happened, is all."

"He can handle himself," Clint said as he turned his attention back to the trail ahead of him. "If there was shooting, we would have heard it. If there was anyone out to kill him, they would have come after us by now as well. Right now, we just need to keep heading west."

"I don't see what you expect from us," Sven grunted. "So you lost a damn horse. Plenty of men lost their horses and they don't feel the need to ride all the way out to hell and back for them. Why don't you just get another one?"

"You really don't think stealing a horse is a serious offense?" Clint scoffed. "I suppose folks just fly off the handle by making laws against it and such. And when it comes to folks in Texas, well they must all just be out of their minds for stringing up horse thieves the first chance they get."

"Texas isn't the only place that does that," Sven said.

"True," Clint replied.

Don let out a tired breath. "Texans are out of their damn minds for plenty of reasons."

"As someone who's spent a good amount of time here, I can tell you that's also true," Clint said. "But punishing horse thieves isn't one of those reasons and both of you know it. All this talk is just a bunch of foolishness from a couple of outlaws trying to justify their actions."

"That's not what Jarred said."

"What was that, Don?"

"Nothing."

Clint shook his head. "I can't believe it. The two of you really did have some kind of moment back in town. What happened? Did you both share an epiphany over a bottle of whiskey?"

"No! Well . . . there was whiskey involved, but not a lot. He was civil and let me have a drink."

"Now there's a man who knows how to treat his prisoner," Sven grumbled.

Clint gnashed his teeth together, wondering if it would be easier to knock them both unconscious or just stuff bandannas in their mouths.

"Jarred said that horse thieves are treated worse than killers," Don continued.

"Is that a fact?" Clint said.

"He said most men care more for their horses than they do for their fellow man."

"Is that a fact?"

"Yes, indeed. He also said that some killers have more of a chance at trial than a horse thief. Every once in a while, a man accused of killing someone may be turned loose. A man accused of stealing a horse is usually strung up right away."

"Is that a fact?"

Don let out an exasperated breath. "You ain't even listening to me."

"I'm listening," Clint said. "I was just checking to see if you were actually hearing what I said or if you were just spouting off about all these convoluted theories of Hall's. By the way, you do know that he's a bounty hunter who'll profit from bringing you in, right? Most likely, it doesn't even matter if you're alive or dead."

"Yeah, I know. He did make some good points, though."

"Then maybe you can discuss them with him," Clint said.

Clint had spotted the rider on the trail ahead a few moments ago and was preparing himself for the worst. Now that they'd closed the distance between each other, he could tell it was Hall galloping straight toward him. The bounty hunter reached him in a short amount of time and fell into step beside Clint.

"What did you find?" Clint asked.

"It was more or less what I thought it would be," Hall replied. "The tracks led off to a good vantage point for scouting. Nobody was there."

"That's good." After a few seconds of silence, Clint looked over at him and studied the other man's face. "What else was there?"

"Not much."

"Did you catch sight of the men we're after?"

Hall shook his head.

"Then what the hell is it?" Clint asked. "It's plain to see there's something wrong."

"I didn't see any of the men we're after, but the spot I did find . . . well . . . it looked like those men probably visited it more than once."

"I don't mean to be cross," Clint said, "but I've had my fill of roundabout talk with these two while you were away. If you've got something to say, just spit it out."

"What I found was a cave," Hall said.

"A cave?"

"That's right."

"You think they used it to hide out or make camp?"

"No." Hall took a deep breath and let it out. "They used it as a grave."

"A grave? For who?"

"For horses."

Clint snapped back on his reins with enough force to make the animal beneath him whinny. After calming the horse down with a few pats to the side of its head, he asked, "There were dead horses?"

"Yeah."

"How many?"

"I didn't stop to count them," Hall explained. "There were a good number, though. Could have been more of them deeper in, but the freshest ones were up front."

"How fresh?"

"Adams, there's no—"

"How fresh, dammit? Answer me!"

For the first time all day, neither of the two prisoners were of a mind to say a word. They held their tongues, doing their best to stay low until this storm blew over.

"I went in to have a closer look," Hall told him. "I wasn't about to count the carcasses or wade in all the way back, but I didn't see any Darley Arabians."

"Are you certain? He's black with a white spot on the nose."

"I'm certain."

Clint let out a relieved breath, but didn't take much comfort from it. "Maybe I should go and look for myself."

"I know what I saw, Adams, and there's no need to turn back. If anything, we should pick up our pace to catch up with these men even sooner. Most of the horses I saw didn't look like they just keeled over of natural causes. They were probably put down for being too cantankerous or otherwise difficult to control during a long ride. There sure as hell weren't that many horses that got sick or broke a leg. I just wanted to prepare you because most Arabians I've ever heard of are rather spirited."

"Yeah," Clint said. "I know. But Eclipse isn't just spirited. He's smart. He'll know when to go along for the sake of saving his own neck."

"That's giving a whole lot of credit to a horse, don't ya think?"

"No," Clint replied sharply. "I think that's giving credit where credit is due."

"All I'm saying is that the cave I found probably isn't the only spot of its kind along these outlaws' route. If we take too long and that horse becomes too much trouble for them . . ."

"I understand," Clint said. "Just look me in the eyes and tell me one more time Eclipse wasn't in there."

"Why would I lie about such a thing?"

"To make certain I stay on this ride to help you get these horse thieves."

Hall met Clint's gaze and said, "He wasn't in there. I checked. I waded deeper into that god awful mess than I wanted to, but I checked."

"All right then. But don't try to argue when I tell you we're riding as late as we can and starting again early in the morning if need be."

"Don't worry," Hall said. "After seeing that cave, I want to find these sons of bitches just as bad as you do."

# Chapter Twenty-Two

The tracks they followed took them straight through the rest of West Texas and across the New Mexico state line. Along the way, there was plenty to see but it wasn't anything Clint or Hall were looking for. Several times, they spotted small groups of riders in the distance, heard shots fired, and even found a few discoveries even more gruesome than Hall's cave.

It was late afternoon on the third day of their ride. Clint took a turn scouting ahead and had fired a shot in the air to catch Hall's attention. When Hall arrived, he found Clint standing near a small cluster of tall trees that bore some very unusual fruit.

"What the hell is this?" Hall asked as he swung down from his saddle.

"Jesus Christ," Don said. "Oh Jesus, I knew it!"

Clint was closest to the tree and had barely had enough time to holster his Colt before the others rode up on him. His eyes were trained on the bodies dangling from the nooses tied to some of the upper branches and his feet did their best to avoid the bodies that were piled on the ground.

"Quiet," Clint said.

Not only did Don keep blabbering, but Sven joined in as well. "Good lord! We gotta turn back," he said. "We can't see this! We gotta turn back."

"You heard the man," Hall said while climbing down from his saddle. "Shut the hell up. Both of you!"

The sight was so terrible and so peculiar that Clint couldn't take his eyes off of it. There were no fewer than seven bodies hanging from the thickest branches of a tree that looked to have been there since the soil itself. They swung back and forth, knocking against each other like wind chimes fashioned from jerked meat. Most of the bodies were unrecognizable due to the amount of flesh that was picked from their bones. Some still wore ragged remains of clothing while others were just bones held together by thick strands of sinew that was too tough to be eaten by the vultures.

"What is this?" Hall asked.

"I don't know," Clint said in a low, reverent tone. "I was hoping you could tell me."

"What's there to tell?" Don cried. "It's a goddamn lynching tree! Are you blind?"

Clint shook his head. "No. This is something else. Something more."

Lowering to one knee, Hall reached down to examine one of the bodies piled on the ground. Those dead men were in even worse condition than the one still dangling from the branches, mainly because not a single one of them was still in one piece. "He's right," the bounty hunter said. "I've seen plenty of lynchings. I've held a few of them. This ain't like anything I've ever seen before."

When Clint looked away from the tree, it wasn't out of disgust. He was looking toward the one man in the group who'd said the least thus far. Sven's eyes were wide and his face was paler than usual. "What's on your mind, Sven?" Clint asked.

Twitching as though he'd just been shaken from a deep sleep, Sven nervously licked his lips. "They're horse thieves."

"How can you tell?"

"Because I've heard about trees like this one here. This is where horse thieves, robbers and any other undesirables are put after they're rounded up."

"Rounded up?" Clint asked.

Before an answer could be given, Don wailed, "There are other trees like this one?"

Sven nodded to both men.

Clint approached the horse shared by the two prisoners so he could pull them both down. At the start of their journey, that had been a cumbersome process. After the last few days of making camp and helping them down for meals and such, he and Hall had it down to a science.

Once Don was down, Clint shoved him toward Hall and said, "Do something to calm him down."

"All right, fella," Hall said as he took hold of Don's elbow. "Let's stretch our legs a bit."

# Chapter Twenty-Three

Once the other two had moved away, Clint untied Sven's ropes. The lanky prisoner's leg wound was healing nicely, but he was still in no condition to make a run for his freedom. Even without the wound, however, he was in no condition to fight.

"Take a breath," Clint told him.

Sven did.

"Now tell me what you know about this."

After steeling himself, Sven said, "I heard that men were rounded up for breaking the rules."

"The rules. You mean the law?"

"Not the government's law. New Mexico's law."

"How's that different?" Clint asked.

"Because the government ain't the one enforcing these rules. When I first heard it, I thought it was just a bunch of talk. You know . . . like a bunch of outlaws sitting around trying to sound like bad men? But these men did more than talk. Now that I see this, I can tell it's a whole lot more."

"Who did all this talking?"

"Victor Howlett, mostly. He said that they did things their own way in New Mexico. That anyone who wants to say any different will get hung out for the vermin to pick their bones. He made it sound pretty bad. But this . . . this is worse than I imagined."

"I thought Howlett was just a horse thief," Clint said.

"He's a thief and a killer. With things getting so bad for thieves in Texas, men like him gotta adapt to survive. That's what he always said."

"What else did he say about this?" Clint asked while pointing to the tree. "And don't give me any tough talk spewed around a campfire."

The glassy look in Sven's eyes was replaced by cold fear which didn't fade in the slightest when he looked away from the tree and over to Clint. "He said that things would start to be handled differently in New Mexico and that soon it would be handled what way in other places too."

"What other places?"

"Everywhere. I'm just telling you what he said. It may have been around a campfire, but it was more than just tough talk. He truly believed it."

Instead of badgering the prisoner, Clint draped an arm around Sven's shoulders and led him away from the tree. After a few steps, they were no longer stepping on crumbled remains. It would take a lot more walking to escape the smell, however.

Calmly, Clint asked, "What did this have to do with bodies swinging from trees?"

"Howlett said that the government's law was no good. That it either punished the wrong men or it didn't punish them the proper way. He'd go on and on about how much better things would be if folks truly knew they couldn't take their chances with a jury that could get it wrong or a judge that could be bought and paid for."

"Vigilantes have been spouting off like that for a mighty long time."

"He wasn't just talking about enforcing the law a different way. He talked about having no law."

"What about those rules you mentioned?" Clint asked.

"Howlett mentioned those, but he didn't exactly dwell on them. What he spoke about more than anything was how folks would either step in line with the way things should be or they'd wind up piled up beneath the hanging trees."

"Go on."

"That's how we'd know when the new world was being forged," Sven said as if he was reciting something he'd committed to memory when he was a child. "The enemies of the righteous would swing for all to see. Those trees would grow from mounds of death and everyone who saw them would know." Sven's eyes had been glassy and not focused on anything in particular. He stared hard at Clint when he added, "They'd know that it was time to either step in line with the new way or be piled up with the rest."

# Chapter Twenty-Four

Clint, Hall and their two prisoners rode the rest of the day in relative silence. After seeing enough dead bodies to turn their stomachs for a year, there simply wasn't a lot for them to say. Their day only got worse after they left that spot. They found two more similar trees that day. The last one showed on the horizon as they were headed toward several narrow columns of smoke rising from what looked to be a large mining camp. Although there were fewer bodies hanging from or stacked beneath the branches of that last tree, there was no mistake that they were put there by the same group.

"You sure it's a bunch of men?" Hall asked as they rode away from the last tree they'd discovered. "It could just be the work of one mad dog killer."

"This is too much killing for one man to do."

"We both know that's not the case, Adams."

"These trees had to be set up fairly recently. Otherwise, someone would have pulled down those bodies and buried them properly."

"We didn't."

Clint flinched at that. "We would have if we didn't have more pressing matters. Time is a factor and I'm not just talking about reclaiming my horse. Sven swears that one of those thieves is connected to what we found today. Wasting time with anything other than tracking them down only lets them get farther away."

"We agree on that much," Hall said. "I noticed something else about them trees. They were all set up more or less the same. Almost like it was some sort of ritual."

"Or a message."

"Yeah. One that's delivered like a club to the back of your head. Someone doesn't want anyone in New Mexico, and they want to make certain that folks are too scared to cross the state line."

"Seems like there's more to it than that," Clint said. "The trees we've found were pretty evenly spaced over several miles. Kind of like a border. Or a line in the sand."

"More like an animal marking its territory," Hall said distastefully.

"Whatever it is, plenty of folk are taking it seriously. Nobody's cleaned up those disgraceful messes. Not the law, nor any concerned citizens. I don't like the sound of that."

"Are you buying all that garbage Sven was trying to sell?"

"It wasn't him selling it," Clint said in a voice that was quiet enough to remain strictly between him and the bounty hunter riding next to him. "He said all that talk came from someone else and I believe him."

"Still doesn't bring us any closer to knowing for certain just what the hell is going on around here. All we had before was rumors, wild stories and speculation. Now we've just got more of it."

"You could say the same thing about following a set of tracks," Clint pointed out. "Use what you've got, make sense out of what you can and wait for it all to point you somewhere."

After mulling that over for a few moments, Hall nodded. "I suppose that makes sense. Better than the alternative, anyway."

"Which is?"

"That we're blindly following a trail marked in blood that any fool in his right mind would avoid."

Clint nodded. "Yeah. I like my version better."

# Chapter Twenty-Five

The camp they'd found consisted of several dozen tents spread over the land that could normally be occupied by a small town. Some of the tents near the center of camp were larger and supported by wooden frames while the ones on the periphery were barely large enough for two people to use for shelter with their feet sticking out from one end. Even if the tracks they were following hadn't led to that place, Clint would have been tempted to stop there for the night.

"You smell what I smell?" Clint asked.

Hall tipped his hat to a small cluster of ladies standing outside one of the larger tents. Judging by the way they were dressed, they were either soiled doves or one hell of a welcoming committee. "I don't smell it yet," Hall said through a leering grin, "but I imagine it's pretty sweet."

"Not that," Clint snapped. "Smells like some of the best cooking I've found in months."

"You chase your pleasures. I'll chase mine."

"Don't forget why we're here."

"I didn't," Hall said. "The last tracks I found were so fresh, I'd wager that wagon is probably parked somewhere in this camp as we speak."

"I'm sure it doesn't hurt that you could sleep on a bed with a warm body next to you instead of stretched out on the ground."

"You're damn right it doesn't. But I'm a professional, Adams. I want to catch these horse thieves just as much as you do."

"All right, then mister professional. I'll let you tend to the prisoners while I put the horses up for the night. My nose is telling me there's some fine supper to be had over in that direction, so I'll meet you there once you get things situated."

There was a wagon parked in the spot where Clint was pointing marked by a banner that read, "Chuck's Eats". Hall glanced back at the prisoners who were gazing about at the camp like dogs watching a steak being dangled in front of them. "We might be better off just parting ways with these two right here," the bounty hunter said.

"And I suppose you know just where to do that?" Clint asked.

"Like you said yourself," Hall proudly replied. "I'm a professional."

Clint studied the people in the vicinity. Most of them fit the description of what he would expect to find in a mining camp. There were ragged men staggering in or out of tents pitched around makeshift saloons, tired prospectors looking for a place to rest their heads, and a variety of men and women looking to profit from them. None of them showed much of any interest in the pair of prisoners that had been brought into town apart from a mild curiosity. On the other hand, Hall seemed just a bit too anxious to rid himself of his burden.

"Tell you what," Clint said. "I'll take Sven and you take Don. That seem fair to you?"

"Christ, Adams. Just give me an hour, huh?"

"No need for this to be so difficult," Clint told him as he climbed down from his saddle.

"Exactly. I . . . hey! What are you doing?"

Clint had walked over to the horse carrying both prisoners and pulled his hunting knife from its scabbard hanging from his belt. "I'm making this easier for both of us," he said. With that, Clint sliced through the rope tying the men to the saddle horn and then made another quick slash that severed the rope tying the prisoners to each other. He roughly pulled Sven down from the saddle and freed his hands.

"You can stick close to me," Clint said to Sven. "And Don can stick close to Jarred. Either that, or the two of you can take your chances out there where horse thieves are getting strung up or left to rot in the dirt. Maybe your friends will still be partial to you. Maybe they won't."

"And why would we have any better chance with you two?" Don asked.

"I'm not after you," Clint said. "When I get what I'm after, if you've proved yourselves, I'd be willing to turn you loose."

Looking to Hall, Don asked, "What about him?"

"I'm after cash," Hall said. "And you two are worth a chunk of it."

Both of the prisoners wilted a bit, but didn't have the spirit to do much about it. Looking for that reaction was almost definitely Hall's reason for saying what he did. Clint was certain of it.

"There are some men at the end of this ride that are worth more, though," Hall added. "They're the same ones that are out for you."

"Out for us?" Sven asked. "What do you mean?"

Seeing exactly where the bounty hunter was headed, Clint pointed to Don and said, "Ask your friend there. He's one of the fellows who tried to gun me down just for showing my face at the wrong time. The man I was with was killed like he was nothing."

"Howlett?" Sven asked.

Don nodded. "Yeah." He then looked to Clint and Hall before shrugging. "Me and Sven know each other. From before."

"Of course you do," Hall sighed. "You both work for the same group doing just about the same thing. You think me and Clint here are idiots for not thinking you two were already acquainted?"

"But nobody ever mentioned anything," Don said.

"What the hell difference does it make?" Clint told him. "I imagine you knew the man I brought with me to set up that meeting with Bennelli."

"Yeah," Don sighed.

"And if those friends of yours were so quick to kill him, then why would they hesitate to kill you two?"

Both men looked at each other and then to Clint. "So what do you want from us?"

Hall approached both of them and put a hand on each one's shoulder. "We just want the two of you to stay healthy. Oh, and the best way to do that is to help us find Bennelli, Howlett and whoever else is behind this insanity."

"How do you figure?" Don chuckled.

"Because with them still out there," Clint said, "you two aren't worth a hill of beans. And in case you haven't noticed those trees we passed on the way here, this ain't exactly friendly territory for the likes of you anymore. Of course, if you'd like to take your chances out there with friends that would just as soon kill you as look at you, go ahead. I'm sick of playing nursemaid."

Neither prisoner had to ponder their choices for very long before Don said, "We're with you, boss. Can we at least have our guns back?"

"Don't push it."

# Chapter Twenty-Six

After parting ways with Clint for the moment, Hall made a beeline to the long tent he'd spotted earlier. It was one of the larger tents supported by a wooden frame and had two water troughs in front of it. In fact, it looked to be one of the largest tents in sight and the business its owners conducted was booming.

Women were lined up in front of the place like so many dresses on display in a seamstress's window. Most of them wore nothing more than slips, flimsy blouses and stockings. There was a wide selection to choose from and the moment he was close enough to see them, Hall was singled out quicker than a piece of raw meat tossed to a pack of dogs.

"This place is great!" he said as he hastened his steps toward the large tent.

"What are we doing here?" Don asked.

"If you have to ask that question after seeing these here ladies, then something ain't right with you."

While all of the ladies were putting on their prettiest smiles, most of them were aimed at Don. Before long, Don was smiling right back at them. "Well, I guess this place is pretty nice," he said.

One of the ladies stepped forward. She was slightly older than the rest, with just a bit more meat on her bones and flowing blond hair. "See anything you like, hon?" she asked.

Don nodded. "I'm looking at her right now."

"Aww, ain't that sweet?" the blonde said. "If I could still blush, I'd be doing it right now. As for your friend," she added while looking over to Hall. "I know exactly what he needs. Andrea! Get on out here!"

A few seconds later, a slender woman with firm, pert breasts walked out of the tent. She was dressed in loose skirts and a corset that pushed her cleavage almost up to her chin. Every step she took caused her to bounce in a way that would catch any man's eye and the smile on her face told Hall that she knew exactly what she was doing.

"I see there's a couple of new faces in the camp," Andrea said. "Which one do I get?"

"This one's mine," the blonde said as she pulled Don close to her ample bosom. Since there was no objection forthcoming, she dragged him into the tent.

Hall stepped forward until he was within inches of Andrea. "Guess that leaves you and me, darlin'."

She smiled, pulled open the tent's flap and showed him inside.

The interior was mostly open space that was sectioned off by folding partitions that divided the rear portion of the tent into rooms. Sounds of other ladies satisfying their customers drifted through the air, mixed with the scents of perfume, cigar smoke and sweat. With Andrea so close to him, however, Hall's senses were quickly filled with nothing but her.

Andrea's long, dark brown hair went all the way down to the small of her back. Her lips were full and naturally red and her body was both soft and muscular. She led him to a room all the way at the back of the tent, situated in a corner that put the main wooden frame on two sides of them. It was the closest thing to real walls they could get, even if the door was just a curtain held shut by a hook set into a loop on the frame.

"Where'd you find that one?" she asked while fitting the hook in place to keep the flap shut.

Hall stood close to her and placed his hands upon Andrea's hips. "He's one of yours, girl. Don't you remember?"

"There's so many, it's hard to keep track."

"Speaking of hard . . ."

As Hall pressed against the front of her body, Andrea reached down between his legs to feel him. When she found his rigid pole, she raised an approving eyebrow. "Isn't it customary to take care of business before pleasure?"

"I've never been one for customs. Besides," he added while taking her firm backside in his hands, "it's been way too long."

# Chapter Twenty-Seven

Andrea wrapped one leg around him and slipped her hands up under Hall's shirt. Raking her fingernails against his bare skin, she whispered, "If you still want a spot in the group, this is a good way to go about it."

"I live to serve, sweet thing."

"I wish I could believe that, Jarred. I really do."

"How would you like me to prove it?"

She backed up a step, pulled the hat off Hall's head and roughly grabbed one of his ears to force him down. Hall didn't do a thing to resist as he lowered himself to his knees in front of her. Andrea lifted her skirts to show that she wasn't wearing a stitch of clothing beneath them and gathered them up around her waist. She then picked one foot up, kicked it out and draped it over one of Hall's shoulders. From there, he wasted no time before reaching around with both hands to cup her ass and pull her close so he could bury his face between her legs.

Andrea smiled widely as she grabbed his hair and arched her back. Hall's mouth found the thatch of hair between her thighs and his tongue slipped inside of her. She ground her hips against his face, moaning softly when he hit just the right spot.

"That's it," she whispered. "God, it has been too long."

He licked her for a while longer and then started to stand back up again. Before he could get to his feet, Andrea gripped his hair and held him where he was. Hall challenged that by standing up anyway until she was forced to let him go. Although she tried to keep him down, she didn't exactly fight. Instead, she gave him a tussle for a few seconds and became even more excited when he grabbed her up in a tangle of arms and legs to lift her off her feet.

Andrea's eyes widened and she pulled in a few excited breaths. When Hall dropped her down onto the cot situated in the middle of the little room, she lay on her back and watched him as he peeled off his clothes. When he loomed over her, she stared at his rigid cock and spread her legs for him.

Hall climbed on top of Andrea and quickly entered her. She was dripping wet and ready for him and when she had every inch of his erection inside, she let out a long, trembling sigh. As the bounty hunter found his rhythm, Andrea propped one leg on the edge of the cot and lifted the other up high. Hall grabbed her ankle so he could bring that leg up close to his mouth and take eager bites along her calf. When he nipped at her a little harder, Andrea watched him intently and writhed beneath him.

"Harder," she whispered.

He fucked her harder, his body pounding against hers amid both of their labored grunts. They weren't the only ones making noise inside that tent, but as far as they both were concerned, they were the only ones that mattered. Andrea rested her leg on Hall's shoulder and leaned back. Closing her eyes tightly, she placed both hands flat upon his chest so she could feel his muscles tense every time he pounded into her.

Soon, Hall pulled out of her and once more put his head between her legs. This time, he didn't tease her before pressing his lips against her pussy and putting his tongue right where it needed to be. Her body reacted out of pure instinct, causing her to spread her legs wide and arch her back as her entire body began to quake. Her climax came quickly and tore through her body in wave after powerful wave. Even before it had subsided, she was getting up and crawling over to him.

Hall lay on the cot, allowing Andrea to claw and bite his flesh wherever she could. She made her way down his chest, along his hips and finally wrapped her lips around his cock. She devoured him greedily, sliding her mouth all the way down to the base of his shaft. From there, Andrea sucked him as though he was her last meal, moaning quietly until he started to buck against her face.

Her mouth curved into a smile and she looked up to see his face as his climax began. Hall took hold of the cot with both hands, clenching his eyes tightly shut and leaning back to savor every moment. Andrea reached up with one hand to run her nails down his chest and used the other to stroke the base of his cock as her tongue went to work on his tip. She licked and tasted him, using her wet mouth to push him all the way over the edge. When he'd finally reached his limit, she closed her lips around him and drank him down.

She kept her mouth on him for a while longer, moaning softly while letting her tongue drift up and down his length. When she was ready, she eased her mouth off of him and settled onto the cot next to the bounty hunter. Draping one leg across his body, she scratched his chest and stomach like a cat that was making its bed.

"Hot damn," Hall sighed. "I sure missed you, Andy."

"Of course you did."

# Chapter Twenty-Eight

Andrea didn't bother getting dressed when she walked across the room to pour drinks for herself and Hall. All she wore was one of the sheets pulled off the cot which hung on her shoulders like a cape. While pouring some whiskey from a bottle into two glasses, she kept her back to Hall.

"So, who is that I saw riding with you into camp?" she asked.

Since all he could see was the back of her head and a wall of white sheet, Hall busied himself with pulling on his clothes. "Don's the man I told you about."

"He was working at my dry goods store in Parker?"

"That's right. The other one who was tied up like a calf at a rodeo worked with Howlett."

"You'll have to be more specific," she said as she turned around. "Victor works with a lot of men."

Now, Hall had something much better to look at. The sheet was still draped over her shoulders, but it provided a backdrop for her naked body. Andrea's skin glistened with the sweat from their lovemaking and her nipples were still erect. The sight of her was enough to pull Hall off the cot and drag him across the room to stand directly in front of her. Taking the glass she offered him, he said, "He rode with one of the groups that went out stealing horses."

"I see. What about the other man? The one who wasn't tied up."

"He's Clint Adams."

"I don't like the tone in your voice when you said that."

Hall drained most of the whiskey from his glass in one sip. "You've never heard that name before?"

"Why would I?"

"He's a well known person. Especially in West Texas."

Andrea sipped her whiskey daintily. Without reacting in the slightest to the alcohol's burn, she shrugged and said, "I've been dealing with a lot of men who claim to be famous. Some of them can back it up while others are just animals who are good at being animals."

"Adams ain't no animal," Hall said.

"Is he a peace officer?"

"Not exactly."

"Then some sort of gunman?"

"Most definitely."

Andrea shrugged again before striding past him to a trunk situated at the foot of the cot. She let her sheet fall off of her, exposing the smooth curves of her waist and hips. "Gunmen don't impress me," she said. "Not anymore."

"He's more than just a gun hand. He's the sort of fellow who sinks his teeth into something and doesn't let go. And when he puts his mind to something, he's deadly enough to see it through all the way to the end."

"Are you trying to frighten me?"

"Nope. Just telling you who those men were that I rode into camp with."

Andrea took another sip of her drink and then bent at the waist to set the glass on the floor. She then opened the trunk and started sifting through the clothes within. "You were sent out with one task," she said. "How is that coming along?"

"Oh, I know how to do my job," Hall told her. "That ain't the problem."

"Then what is the problem, exactly?" she snapped. The edge on her tone was more than enough to overcome the fact that she was standing naked before him. In fact, Hall even backed away from her out of pure instinct as she glared at him.

"You were sent out to work for the cause," she continued. "Why haven't you delivered yet?"

"I brought the money. What bothers me more is them trees scattered out there. And don't you dare try batting your eyelashes and telling me you don't know what I'm talking about."

"Why are you so surprised, Jarred? Many of the men hanging from those trees were men you brought to us over the past month."

"If I'd known they'd end up like that . . ."

"You'd do what?" she asked. "Notify the sheriff? Bring a marshal to this camp? Good luck finding either. There's no real law to be found throughout all of New Mexico. In case you'd forgotten, that was part of the plan as well."

"And what part of the plan mentioned stringing up human beings like they was nothing but meat?"

Andrea selected a plain green dress and slipped it on. "We're sending a message," she told him. "Several, actually. The lawmen will know that their rules no longer apply here and the lawless will know that there's a new authority that must be reckoned with. For everyone else who happens upon those trees, those trees will serve as fair warning that changes are coming and that they'll be written in blood."

"I suppose that was Howlett's idea?" Hall said. "Something that disgusting reeks of that little mongrel."

"It was his idea. Funny that you never seemed to mind working with him before. I believe you knew about his nature well before I was even introduced to him."

"Knowing about a murderous animal is one thing. Giving him free rein to smear his filth all over the place is something else."

Andrea was still quite a sight. Although the dress was a simple garment that could be found at any store, she wore it as provocatively as the sheet she'd just cast onto the floor. The front was meant to be laced up, but she hadn't gotten around to that. Beads of sweat ran down the front of her body, forming a shimmering line between her pert breasts. The fabric clung to every inch of her body in a way that promised at the pleasures she could give once she peeled it off again.

"There's no reason for you to be so upset," she told him.

"I ain't upset."

"Really?"

"The plan was to set things up in New Mexico so folks like you, me and Howlett can do as we please," Hall said. "We needed cash, so I've been getting it while the rest of you set up shop here."

"Setting up shop means breaking down the institutions holding this entire country hostage," Andrea snapped. "Law, government, morality, all of it has to be weakened before anarchy can take root. Once the seed is planted, it can only grow once it is out there for all to see. Just like our little trees," she told him with a smile.

"That's real clever. Who came up with that one? Far-raday?"

"Why yes. Our Mister Farraday is full of plenty of good ideas. One of those ideas was to take full advantage of the successes we've had by expanding our operation."

"Expanding?" Hall asked warily. "By how much?"

"You're not the only man we sent out to collect for us. Admittedly, you are the most successful. One thing we found was that our efforts to fertilize the bounty market brought some attention to me and Farraday."

Hall let out an exasperated breath. "I warned you about that. God damn it."

"Actually that turned out fairly well. Most of the men who came here to follow up with us decided to join our cause."

"What cause is that? Last I checked, we were all just out to make some quick cash."

"Oh, it's gotten much larger than that," Andrea said. "Using all the extra hands we've managed to draw under our banner, we've been able to erode a good amount of confidence people used to have in the government and the laws that can no longer protect them."

Hall examined her through narrowed eyes. When he spoke, it was in a hushed tone. "The cause? Rallying under a banner? You sound more like a bunch of damned revolutionaries."

She matched his tone, but more out of excitement instead of any sense of nervousness. "That's exactly what we are, Jarred. It's very exciting and it's all a lot easier than you might expect. When was the last time you were in Parker?"

"A couple days ago."

"If we wanted, we could ride in and take over that town. Or, if we were in a different mood, we could burn it to the ground and divert the survivors to any location we chose."

"Listen to yourself," Hall said. "What the hell are you proposing?"

"It's not just me."

"You and Farraday, then."

Andrea nodded. "When he told me about his new plan, I didn't believe it could possibly work. But the beautiful part is that it doesn't have to completely work in order to succeed. Even just a few scattered victories would be enough to make us wealthy. Any more than that will make us legends."

"All right, then," Hall said calmly. "Let's hear it."

She told him and when she was through, Hall knew that all the bodies he and Clint had found on the way into the camp was nothing compared to what was to come.

# Chapter Twenty-Nine

Clint sat at a table fashioned from three uneven pieces of lumber and what looked like the back side of an old bookcase. Despite the furnishings, however, the food was just as good as it smelled. The plate in front of him was mostly clean, but there were a few stray pieces of flaky pie crust and filling left. He used a fork to scrape it off while Sven sat across from him working on a hunk of pot roast and several halved potatoes.

The lanky fellow with the bandaged leg sat hunched over his food as if he was afraid someone was going to steal it right out from under his nose. He was speaking to Clint in a hurried whisper when Hall stepped inside the tent. Since there was about half as much space in the whole restaurant as there had been in the cathouse's makeshift parlor, Hall had no problem finding the men he was after.

"Well now," Hall said as he crossed the room to march straight over to Clint's table. "This place does some of the best business in town."

Clint looked up at him with an easy smile. "Why don't you pull up a chair? I recommend the chicken and dumplings. Best in the country, I'm told."

"Yeah, well cooks say a lot of wild things about their own food. Still, I'm real hungry."

"I'll bet you are," Clint said. "You were at that cathouse for a while."

Winking, Hall said, "I always ask for seconds. Know what I mean?"

"Course I do. Sven, why don't you take the Remington from Jarred's holster?"

"What's the meaning of this?" Hall asked.

Clint shifted in his seat so Hall could see that his hand was already on the grip of his Colt. "I'd ask you to hand over your gun on your own, but thought that might make you a little suspicious. And don't think about using our friend there as any kind of shield. I'd just as soon shoot through him as push him aside. No offense, Sven."

"None taken," Sven replied. He already had the Remington in hand and quickly sat back down in his chair. "Where do you want this?"

Clint kept his eyes on Hall and his voice calm when he replied, "Just drop it on the floor."

The pistol made a solid thump when it hit the boards that had been laid directly onto packed dirt. After that, Sven didn't seem to know quite what to do with himself so he placed his hands upon the table.

"Why don't you tell Jarred where you spent your evening," Clint said.

Reluctantly, Sven said, "I . . . meant to stay with Mister Adams here, but then I thought it sounded better to . . . well . . . I thought I might take some time for myself with one of them ladies we saw on our way into camp."

Hall pulled in a deep breath.

"And after I was through," Sven continued, "I was left to show myself out and along the way, I couldn't help overhearing you talking to another one of them ladies."

"Shit," Hall said as he let out the breath he'd been holding.

"Yeah," Clint said. "Something like that. Why don't you tell me what you and that lady talked about?"

"Why should I bother? I imagine that idiot there already told you everything," Hall said.

"He told me plenty. But if what you tell me doesn't line up with what he told me, then I'll know one of you is lying."

"And where would you go from there?" Hall asked. "Gun one of us down while these fine folks are in the middle of eating their pie?"

There were only three other people inside the tent with food on their plates and none of them took notice that Clint or anyone else at that table were drawing breath.

"What's the matter?" Clint asked. "Nervous?"

"When shots may be fired at me for something someone else already told you? Yeah. You're damn right I'm nervous. Tell me one thing, though. If you do get a reason to be suspicious, how will you decide which man to blame?"

"Simple. I'll use my gut."

After hardly any consideration, Hall nodded. "That's good enough for me."

# Chapter Thirty

"The whore I went to in that cathouse is named Andrea Bennelli," Hall announced.

"Andrea," Clint said. "As in Andy Bennelli?"

"One and the same."

"So you knew she was here?" Clint asked.

"Not as such. I knew she'd be in the area. You see, she drifts around between here and several other camps and towns in a couple of different counties. Parker included, of course. She runs that dry goods store and plenty others like it in those other places."

"Always dry goods stores, huh?" Clint asked suspiciously.

"Well, not always."

Since he already knew what kind of goods were sold at the place where Andrea worked in that camp, Clint moved along without dwelling on Hall's activities there. "Sven told me you had a lengthy conversation with her. What was it about?"

"Look, Adams. I'm not about to waste our time by telling you something you've already been told. When I signed on to this outfit, it was for the same reason that I take any other job: money. These people running this show had a good way to make men in my line of work rich."

"That's what I want to know," Clint said. "Who's running this show? For that matter, what is the damn show?"

Ticking off his fingers one by one, Hall recited, "Andy Bennelli, Victor Howlett and someone named Farraday. They're the ones calling the shots. When this all started, it was a simple scheme. They knew plenty of outlaws and horse thieves, which they turned loose on different ranches and such. After a bit of time passed, men like me would hunt them down and cash in the reward."

"That's not a new scheme," Clint said.

"No, it ain't. That's why I didn't think much of it when I signed on. These sorts of things usually pay off real well, but the trick is knowing when to step away. They tend to get real messy real fast and when they go up in flames, everyone takes a fall."

"So did you also ride back to break these outlaws out of jail?"

"Nope. And I doubt anyone had that job because I saw some of 'em swinging from those trees we passed on the way in."

"If these three know these outlaws they're using, why hand them over to bounty hunters?" Clint asked.

"You'd have to ask them that," Hall replied. "All I can tell you is that none of these outlaws were friends with them three I mentioned. If they was, then I sure as hell don't want to know how they treat their enemies."

Clint pointed across the table at Sven, who seemed more than happy to stay out of the conversation altogether. "He mentioned something about more blood being spilled and that Bennelli wanted you to help burn down a couple towns."

"That's what I wanted to tell you, Adams! Things may have started off as just a bunch of like-minded sorts getting together to make some fast money, but they ain't gonna end that way. Them three got a taste of what they could accomplish and they're not about to pull back."

"What power?"

"It started when a posse was formed to go after some of those horse thieves when they were spotted riding back to one of their hideouts. No bounty had been collected yet and they weren't about to give up a good chance to rake in some of that cash."

"Who are you talking about? Bennelli and Farraday?"

"No. Howlett. He rides with a small group of men, but it ain't hardly ever the same men more than once. He usually prefers the company of real bloodthirsty types and they tend to get into a lot of shooting fights. Howlett is usually the only one to walk away from 'em."

"That's because Howlett isn't above killing them himself," Sven said. When he spoke, both Clint and Hall seemed surprised to hear him make any noise.

"Howlett kills his own men?" Clint asked.

"That's the word," Sven said. "Nobody can prove it, though, because nobody survives any of those incidents."

"I wouldn't doubt it," Hall said. "Howlett's got more bugs in his head than…well…he's crazy is what he is. Him shooting his own men or his own brother doesn't seem out of character for an animal like that. Anyway, Howlett and his boys got a hold of this posse and burned every last one of them off the face of the earth. It was so bad that nobody wanted to step in and take that lawman's place."

"So that town just went without a peacekeeper?" Clint asked.

"That's right. And it wasn't the only one. Howlett bein' Howlett, he decided to run the same thing on another town. This time, he was all excited about the prospect of what might happen and he slaughtered the next set of lawmen even worse than the first. Same result, though. Ain't no man about to sign up for the job of hunting him down."

"That's not a new scheme either," Clint sighed.

"What's new is where this scheme is headed," Hall said. "And this is where Farraday comes in. He's gotten it into his head that the law can be run out of New Mexico altogether."

"Out of the whole state?"

"Yeah. Not only has he turned Howlett loose like some kind of wild dog, but he'd recruited other killers to ride in his name. Carrying his banner, so to speak."

"Usually killers like Howlett aren't concerned with waving banners or anything along that line," Clint said, speaking from his own experience. "They're after money or just the thrill of the hunt. They concern themselves with their reputation, but that's got nothing to do with sending men out to do things for them."

"And this ain't got a thing to do with Howlett's reputation," Hall insisted. "It's about Farraday staking a claim on all of New Mexico."

"What kind of nonsense is that?" Clint asked.

"You can believe me or not, Adams. I'm just tellin' you what I heard straight from the source. This territory is wild enough on its own. All these killers had to do was make it seem even wilder and the whole thing can come off its rails. We've both seen it!"

"But what would anyone think to do once they did take New Mexico?"

Hall shook his head slowly. "I don't profess to know how a crazy man's head works. What I do know is that if he can't take it for himself, Farraday intends to make it a hell all its own."

# Chapter Thirty-One

"This is a bad idea, Adams." When he realized Clint wasn't paying him any mind, Hall stepped in front of him and planted his feet. "Stop! Will you listen to me?"

"I've done enough listening. It hasn't gotten me anywhere."

It had been a matter of seconds since Clint had left the restaurant. As soon as Hall had told him about the chaos that was about to be unleashed, he'd stood up from the table and stormed outside. Sven had hobbled along behind him and Hall tried to follow. Judging by the angry voices behind him, Clint figured the bounty hunter was held up by the restaurant owner demanding to be paid for the food that had been served. Hall settled the bill one way or the other before charging out of the tent to try and bring Clint to a stop. He'd succeeded for the moment, but was shoved aside the moment following that.

"Get in my way again," Clint warned, "and I'll assume you're one of the bastards trying to separate me from what I came for."

Hall moved aside rather than fight Clint then and there. Falling into step beside him, he said, "This is about a lot more than some damn horse. Can't you see that?"

Without breaking stride, Clint turned his head to fix a deathly glare on Hall. The bounty hunter held up his hands and quickly added, "Okay, he's more than a damn horse. I understand. But you've got to believe me that these people are serious. They may be a bunch of god-damn loons, but they're serious!"

"I understand both of your points," Clint said. "Those trees we found made your case rather nicely."

"Right, so we need to tread lightly here."

"Why?"

"Why?" Hall gasped. "What the hell do you mean why? Sometimes it seems like we're on the same page and then sometimes it seems like you ain't even listen-ing."

"There's listening and obeying," Clint said. "Just be-cause I do one doesn't mean I'm obliged to do the other. Besides, if I did that, Lord only knows what would happen."

"And what's that supposed to mean?"

Clint didn't bother answering. He just kept right on walking until Hall circled around to plant himself direct-ly in his path again. There was plenty of space on the street to go around, but Clint knew that would only prompt him to make the same play again.

"Out of my way," Clint warned.

"Or what?" Hall asked defiantly.

"Or I'll move you."

Clint's eyes narrowed into angry slits. Before he could say what was on his mind, Sven put himself between the other two men. "Let's not start fighting among ourselves," the lanky horse thief said.

"Too late for that," Hall growled.

Clint nodded.

"Maybe we've all just gotten wound up," Sven offered. "We don't seem to be thinking clearly."

"Why do you say that?" Clint asked.

"Does anyone even know where Don is?"

Locking eyes with Hall, Clint replied, "I'm guessing I'll find him when I pay a visit to that whorehouse."

"That's where you're going?" Hall said.

"Of course it is. That's where I'll find Andy Bennelli, right?"

"Yes. Wait! You're just going to march in there and confront Andy Bennelli?"

"After you told me who she was and where she was, did you honestly expect me to do anything other than that?" Clint replied.

"What I thought is that you'd listen to what I had to say and then take a moment to think about what it means," Hall said.

Crossing his arms, Clint said, "All right, then. What does it mean? Tell me. You've got five seconds."

"You're being unreasonable, Adams."

"Four seconds."

"Should we really be doing this in the middle of the damn street?" Hall asked.

"Three seconds."

"This is bigger than just a horse, no matter how attached anyone may be to that horse. Men are dying and there are bloodthirsty savages out there ready to kill more. The law ain't about to get involved because somehow they've already been handled and if things keep going this way, all of New Mexico might just fall into anarchy! Doesn't that even make a dent in that stubborn head of yours?"

Clint's only reply to that was, "Time's up." He then shoved Hall aside and kept walking straight through the middle of the camp as if he had an entire army behind him.

"Should we go after him?" Sven asked.

"Eh, to hell with him," Hall replied with a dismissive wave of his hand. "If he wants to sign his own death warrant, then I'm inclined to let him."

# Chapter Thirty-Two

When Clint stepped into the large tent, he was greeted by a rail-thin woman with black hair and a pretty face. "Hello, handsome," she said through a painted smile. "See anything you like?"

"Andrea Bennelli," Was Clint's crisp reply.

"Are you a friend of hers?"

"Not yet, but I'm very anxious to make her acquaintance."

The slender girl turned to look at a rough looking man behind her. He shook his head and posted himself in the doorway leading to the rest of the tent. Turning her attention back to Clint, the skinny woman said, "She's not available, but I'm sure I or one of the other girls can take good care of you."

"She's back there?" Clint asked. The skinny girl twitched and shifted on her feet, which prompted Clint to move straight ahead. "I'll just show myself around."

He made it to the man who'd been standing there like a specter and glared directly into his eyes. "Step aside, mister," Clint snarled. "You're not frightening me just by taking up space."

The man bared his teeth, perhaps to say something, but wasn't able to do much else before Clint snapped his head forward to connect with the bridge of that man's nose. It wasn't a hard knock, but it certainly rattled him enough for Clint to get past him without any further difficulty.

As soon as Clint stepped through that doorway, a big fellow with fists like thickly knotted rope emerged from one of the little rooms in the rear portion of the tent. Clint stopped and looked at him. "Can you take me to Andy Bennelli?"

Obviously not hired as any sort of guide, the man brought his fists up and took a couple of long strides toward Clint. He took a swing with enough steam behind it that Clint could feel the breeze as he leaned back to let it pass him by. If the swing had connected, it might have sent Clint sailing out of the tent completely. Since it met no resistance whatsoever, the punch took the man off his balance and sent him staggering for half a step. That was more than enough for Clint to pick his shot. The one he chose was a quick jab to the side of the other man's face which caught him between his nose and upper lip. The man's head snapped to one side and he continued staggering until he became tripped up by his own feet. When that man toppled face-first into another room, Clint was already on his way further into the tent.

"Andy Bennelli!" he shouted. "I just want a word with you."

The flap separating yet another room from the hall snapped open directly to Clint's left. A stout fellow holding a sawed-off shotgun took quick aim and thumbed back his hammers. Clint's hands were even faster as they wrapped around the barrel of the shotgun, twisted, and pulled the weapon away from its owner. In one swift movement, Clint swung the shotgun straight back around to crack it against the side of the stout man's head. The shotgun's previous owner blinked a few times and stumbled out of sight once the flap closed again.

"Andy Bennelli!" Clint shouted. "I'd hate to drive away all these paying customers!"

Whether or not that threat made the difference, the flap at the end of the row was pulled aside so Andrea could show herself. "You think you can just walk in here, kill my men and have a conversation with me?"

"None of those men are dead. What do you think I am?" Clint asked. "Some kind of animal that would murder someone and put them on display? Oh, sorry about that. I was talking about someone else."

"Just who do you think you are?"

"I'm Clint Adams."

"Is that supposed to mean something to me?"

"Your men stole my horse and I want it back."

Opening her arms to grant Clint a clear view of her body, she said, "Do I look like a horse thief to you?"

"No, but looks can be deceiving. I have it on good authority that you are associated with the men who stole my horse and several others. Now this whole thing has become a much bigger mess than I would have anticipated so if you'll just return what was taken from me, I can be on my way."

"I don't know about any horses that were taken."

"So you want me to believe that you're not associated with Victor Howlett? He was seen coming and going from this camp as well as this very tent more than once."

"My girls and I entertain many men," Andrea replied.

"What about Farraday?" Clint asked. "Keeping company with the likes of him can be awfully dangerous."

Andrea sighed and rolled her eyes. "There may have been someone named Howlett that came through here," she said. "As for Farraday, you have no idea how dangerous he can be."

"The man you need to worry about is me," Clint warned. "If you thought Texas was tough on horse thieves, you haven't considered what I'm ready to do to anyone who harms one hair on my horse's head. It's been a hell of a long couple of days. I'm tired. Help me get my horse or I'll take out some more of my aggressions."

"There were some horses out back," Andrea said.

"Were there?"

"And a cart."

Clint's first instinct was that she was simply trying to get him out of her sight. But when she mentioned the cart, he figured there could have been some truth to it. Besides, if he wasn't going to listen to what she'd said, it would have been a waste of time storming in there in the first place.

The men that he'd knocked around on his way to have his talk with Andrea were starting to get to their feet. Some of the others inside that tent were taking an interest in him as well. Those things, along with the realization that he may have acted a little quickly, all drifted to the top of Clint's mind as he backed away from Andrea. After taking one more step, he bumped into someone. Clint wheeled around, ready to either defend himself or apologize. But the man he found wasn't trying to toss him out and he wasn't a customer.

"Don?" Clint said.

"I saw your horse, Mister Adams," Don said. "Black Darley Arabian, right?"

"Yes."

Don pointed to the front of the tent and when Clint glanced in that direction, a heavy blow was delivered to a spot directly behind Clint's ear.

Everything went black and Clint was out before he hit the ground.

# Chapter Thirty-Three

Clint had been knocked cold several times in his life. In fact, he'd heard someone once say that any man who hadn't been knocked down more than once hadn't lived a very exciting life. He couldn't recall who'd said that, but when Clint woke up, he also couldn't recall what he'd had for breakfast.

His head was throbbing so badly that he wondered if his skull had been split apart like an egg. He felt everything spinning around him. After taking a few steadying breaths, the sensation lessened to the point where he felt more like the ground was just pitching back and forth beneath him. He took a few more breaths, which did nothing to make him feel any better. Before allowing himself to worry about his health, he took a moment to try and figure out what he was hearing.

There were muffled noises coming from all around. They droned in a thumping, irregular rhythm. There were also creaks, breaths and the occasional splash. Clint tried to move and found he couldn't. Not much, anyway. He could flex his hands and when he did, his fingers scraped against rough wood. He heard an impact of something cracking against something else, which was followed by everything around him shifting from side to side.

He was in a wagon.

His hands were tied.

He was moving.

Of those things he could be certain. Clint listened harder for a bit longer to put a few more pieces together.

The cart he was in wasn't very big. Clint's eyes were covered, but he could tell by the way the sounds rattled inside that there wasn't much space. He confirmed that by stretching out his legs only to have his boots knock against a wall before he could straighten them all the way. Since his ankles weren't bound together, he spread his legs and kicked out to either side with both feet to see if he could find any other barriers around him.

His left leg tapped against a wooden wall almost immediately. His right thumped against something as well, but it wasn't made of wood.

"Hey," a familiar voice hissed. It came from only a foot or so away.

"Who is that?" Clint asked, trying to sound fierce instead of surprised by the discovery.

"I . . . I don't..."

"Sven? Is that you?"

"Y-yeah."

"Tell me what's going on," Clint said. "Now."

"How should I know?" Sven replied in a vaguely trembling voice. "I'm tied and blindfolded. I didn't even know anyone else was in here until you started squirming."

"How long have we been in this cart?"

"I don't know. I was knocked out at that camp and when I woke up, I was here. That was a half hour ago. Maybe less. I can't really say for certain."

With every second that passed, Clint felt more of his strength returning. He pulled against the ropes tying his wrists together, but could barely get himself any slack. When he leaned forward, he realized those same ropes had been threaded through something embedded within the floor itself.

"Can you move?" Clint asked.

"I've been trying, but haven't had much success."

"This feels like a prison cart. Probably rings in the floor meant for shackles to be threaded through."

"Could be a wagon," Sven offered. "We could even be in a box or crate of some kind."

"No," Clint said. "It's a wagon. The same wagon we've been following since leaving Parker."

"Are you sure about that?"

"Pretty much. It feels like it's about the size of the one we were after. There's no way for me to be absolutely certain just yet, but it makes sense."

Sven sighed. "Yes. I suppose it does. It also makes sense that we'll end up hanging from one of those trees with all the bodies piled around them."

"Only if we give in. They want something from us," Clint said, mostly as a way to air out his own thoughts. "Otherwise they would have killed us already. It's a lot easier to store two bodies instead of worrying about tying up two live ones."

"What about Don and Mister Hall? You think they're in here with us? You think maybe they were killed and left somewhere?"

"Don played a part in putting me into this cart," Clint replied. "My guess is that he's the one that knocked me out. As for Hall, I'd say he probably had a hand in us being here as well."

"Never trust a bounty hunter," Sven said in a voice that had an uncharacteristically rough edge to it. "At least an outlaw has some loyalties. Bounty hunters don't know what loyalty is."

"We'll see about that." As the cart rolled to a stop, Clint added, "And we probably won't have to wait very long."

# Chapter Thirty-Four

The first thing Clint thought when he heard the back of the cart being opened was that he had to watch his step. Even if he couldn't understand what was being said by the men outside, the tension in their voices was high and the metallic clicks of pistols being cocked were unmistakable. The back of the wagon was opened, unleashing a swarm of movement as Clint was threatened, pushed face-down against the floor, freed from the ropes and held down with several boots to his back and neck.

"Don't you move!" someone snarled. "We got you covered. Try to run and you'll be cut in half!"

The threats continued along those lines while Clint was dragged out of the cart, forced to his knees outside and tied up again. From the sound of it, Sven was getting fewer threats and more of a beating. Thumps of fists and boots raining blows down onto him were punctuated by pained grunts and moans from the lanky horse thief.

"Take off them blindfolds," said someone with a voice that sounded like wet gravel being forced through a sieve.

Clint didn't realize just how tight the blindfold had been until it was roughly pulled off of him. Sunlight hit his eyes to blind him momentarily. When he opened his eyes for a few quick blinks, he thought he might be blinded even longer. His sight returned in drips and drabs, telling him that it was even later in the day than he'd previously guessed.

"So you're Clint Adams, huh?" the man with the gravelly voice said. "I heard'a you."

"Well I'm real honored," Clint dryly replied.

The light flooding Clint's vision was eclipsed by a solid figure and the breath he'd just taken was forced from his lungs by a solid kick to the gut. Clint doubled over and stayed there for longer than he needed. Not only did that buy him a few more seconds to catch his breath, but it made whoever had hit him think he'd done more damage.

"I thought maybe you were just one of those men who claim to have made a name for himself," the other man said as he placed his heel on Clint's shoulder and pushed him down. "Looks like I was right about that. No man with that kind of reputation is brought down so easy."

Clint knew better than to buy into such an obvious taunt, but he wasn't about to lie down and play dead like a common dog. He shrugged the other man's boot off of him and propped himself up so he could look up at the men surrounding him. There were five of them that he could see. The one closest to him was the one who'd tried to keep Clint under his boot. Victor Howlett's features were just as rough as the last time Clint had seen them. In fact, they may have seemed even more savage now that he was focused entirely on his prey.

"Ahh," Howlett sneered as he looked directly into Clint's eyes. "There's the fire I was expectin' to find. Looks like you may be Adams after all."

"What if I am?" Clint asked.

"Then it means we was right to keep you alive. There are some folks that'd like to have a word with you."

"I've got some words for you, but I don't think you're going to like them."

Howlett grinned before snapping his foot forward to send Clint once more to the dirt. "Yeah, I bet you do. Say all you want, Adams. The less breath you have in yer lungs, the easier it'll be to make the rest of this ride."

"How much farther do we have to go?" Clint asked.

"Not much. Thought you might want to stretch yer legs, though."

Clint took a look around at the rest of the men surrounding him and Sven. One of them stood well over six feet tall and had more hair than a mangy dog. A thickly muscled torso, trunk-like arms and massive fists marked him as someone Clint did not want to trade punches with unless there was absolutely no alternative. Another man was about Clint's height and had a lean build. He had long hair as well, but it was straighter and darker, framing a sunken face with sharply angular, Asian features. His stringy black mustache and beard resembled oil that was dripping off his face.

The man standing near the front end of the cart was clean-shaven and carried a rifle cradled in the crook of one arm. Like all the others, he wore a holster buckled around his waist. Unlike the others, however, he had a gut that was big enough to almost cover his buckle. The last man in sight was the only one wearing a mask. He was dressed in jeans and a waistcoat over a dark blue shirt. The shotgun in his hands was held at waist level but pointed toward Clint and Sven.

"You can drop the air of mystery, Andrea," Clint announced. "And you might as well drop the mask too. It's not fooling anyone."

The man holding the shotgun reached up to peel the scarf down from his face to reveal that Clint had indeed been correct. Smiling, Andrea asked, "How did you know?"

"I might have taken a good knock to the head," Clint told her, "but I can still recognize a woman's curves even if they are wrapped in a set of men's clothes."

"There's a creek right over there," she said while nodding away from the cart. "You should refresh your-self for the rest of the ride."

"Don't mind if I do."

# Chapter Thirty-Five

The stream was on the other side of a short row of trees that blocked most of the water from Clint's sight. His head was still aching from being knocked out and more recently blinded by one hell of a bright day. Those things were quickly fading, however, and the fresh air was doing him plenty of good.

"I take it Sven doesn't get to refresh himself?" Clint said.

"He'll be along later. I want some time to talk to you."

"Oh, so you didn't pull me out of that cart just so I could splash some water on my face?"

"No," she replied through a little smirk.

"What a surprise. Then I guess this is the part where you try to find out what I know regarding your little enterprise. Or perhaps you're interested in where to find the man who was riding with me. In the interest of saving some time, I'll tell you the answers are not much and I don't know."

"You sure do like to hear yourself talk," Andrea mused.

"I have no qualms with keeping quiet."

Behind them, the cart was being tended by most of the men who'd been there to drag Clint and Sven into the daylight. The ones who weren't seeing to the cart or the horses pulling it were keeping an eye on Clint and Andrea. Sven was being questioned by Howlett and so far, it seemed to be relatively painless for the lanky thief.

As they kept walking, Clint could hear movement ahead of them. He guessed there were at least a few more men already at the stream. Clint's hand drifted toward his hip out of reflex. He was surprised to find his holster still there. It was less of a surprise that the holster was empty.

"I'm surprised you didn't guess what I wanted to talk about right away," Andrea said.

"So why don't you tell me?"

"To see if you'd like to join us, of course."

"And what is it about me that makes you think I'm the sort of man who would enjoy stringing human beings up from trees like animal carcasses?"

"Nothing," she replied. "Nothing at all. You must realize that those trees were just signposts marking our territory."

"So those are scattered all along the New Mexico border?"

"More or less. But the movement involves a lot more than that. There are lawmen that have either been turned to our cause or killed outright. The same could be said for outlaws and even several legitimate businesses."

"That doesn't mean a whole lot," Clint said. "Lawmen have been killed or gone bad ever since the first badge was pinned onto someone. Outlaws die or join up with new gangs. That's just what they do. And Businessmen?" Clint laughed. "I've found that men in fancy suits who sit behind expensive desks have backed more outlaws than anyone."

"What makes us different from them is simple," Andrea told him. "They work within the former structure of laws and government."

"Former?"

Andrea nodded. "That's right. What we've been doing is showing folks that there is no law that can stand up against enough people who refuse to follow it. In these recent days, it has been made perfectly clear that there is no law worth following in New Mexico."

"I don't suppose any of you have bothered to wonder what might happen once the government decides to move against you."

"They already have. Lawmen have been sent and they've either decided to join us or decorate one of our trees to send word of what happens to anyone who takes up arms against us."

"Beyond the law, then," Clint said. "What about the Army? There's probably a regiment or two right now looking for a target that's ripe for some cannon fire."

Andrea merely shrugged. "They won't find any targets other than a few scattered outlaws and crooked lawmen. I doubt the President will allow another war to take place within this country without more of a threat than that."

"You don't think those trees you're all so proud of will incite some action?"

"Some," she admitted, "but not enough. People with rules to follow and laws binding them tend to move rather slowly. By the time any sort of action is taken here, our movement will have already spread."

"Spread where?" Clint asked.

Andrea smiled and stepped between two of the trees that had been acting as a natural barrier between the trail and the stream. "That's the sort of thing I might talk about once I know I can trust you. For now, here's a token to show you we can be very good allies to have."

When Clint saw what was waiting for him, he very nearly kissed Andrea full on the lips.

# Chapter Thirty-Six

"Eclipse!"

Clint didn't want to let his cards show in front of his captors, but the reaction was difficult to contain. Seeing the Darley Arabian drinking from the stream was enough to make all of the hell from the last few days worth it in Clint's mind. He rushed over to the stallion without giving a thought to the man who stood nearby watching over it and the other horse being watered.

The man had a rifle in his hands and started to bring it to his shoulder. He must have gotten a signal from Andrea because he nodded, lowered the rifle and took a step back.

As soon as he felt Eclipse's coat against his palm, Clint felt like himself again. The notion of hopping onto Eclipse's back and bolting away from the stream crossed his mind, but he didn't want to risk any harm coming to a companion that had already been through so much.

"How are you, boy?" he said quietly while checking the stallion for wounds.

"He's fine," Andrea said. "We've been treating him very well."

"I wasn't asking you," Clint snapped.

"Watch yer goddamn mouth," one of the armed men nearby warned.

Clint ignored him as he continued examining Eclipse. "Looks like he's alright," he said. Turning to face the man who'd just spoken, he added, "Which is a good thing because anything that happened to him would've happened to any son-of-a-bitch who was responsible."

Andrea stepped forward. "We may steal horses, but we don't harm them."

"What about the horses that wound up slaughtered in a cave outside of Parker? You gonna tell me all of them broke a leg?"

"No," she said. "Some were wounded by stray gunfire. Others wouldn't do what they were trained to do. Plenty of men have died for the same reasons lately."

Rather than trade threats with her, Clint said, "I'm glad to see my horse again. That doesn't mean I'm grateful or indebted to the ones that stole him in the first place. You must really take me for some kind of fool if you think this would sway me over to your side."

Andrea approached him slowly. When she reached out to touch him, she seemed both anxious to get her hands on Clint's chest and nervous about what might happen once she did. "Far from it," she told him. "I think you're a very smart man. That's why I'm being so honest with you."

She was closer to him now. So close that Clint could feel the heat from her body and the touch of her breath against his face when she spoke in a whisper that was so soft he could barely hear it.

"You know what I tell most of the men who join up with us?" she asked. "That we can make them rich. That we will give them some measure of revenge against the law or whatever rich folks they despise. Pretty much anything we think will appeal to them and it's not that difficult to figure out. The only truly interesting part is how many of them don't know they're being fed—"

"Bullshit," Clint said. "You're feeding a bunch of killers bullshit."

"Exactly."

"And you say that like you're so proud of yourself."

"You haven't been riding through the reformed New Mexico for very long," Andrea said. "Surely you must have already seen how much has changed. And don't bother mentioning the trees, Mister Adams. I'm not a fool either. I know a man like you isn't nearly as squeamish as you're letting on."

"True. What's your point?"

Taking a step back, Andrea put her hands on her hips and brought her voice up to a pitch that someone might use if they were campaigning for office. "My point is that we've done a lot here in a short amount of time and we've only gotten started. When the fire gets stoked even higher, you're going to want to be on the right side of it when the wind starts to blow."

"And that side is yours?" Clint asked.

"Yes, Mister Adams. It is. Right now, I'm your best chance at making it out of this alive. You might want to remember that when you're speaking to me and show some of the proper goddamn respect."

"Now there's the tone of a murderous revolutionary. I was starting to wonder if you were just the whore that was dangled in front of prospective recruits to get them to throw in with this Farraday's cause."

"Trust me," Andrea purred. "Mister Farraday wouldn't have tolerated your guff for nearly as long as I have and frankly, I'm surprised Howlett hasn't gutted you yet."

"I actually thought he would have tried by now as well."

"He will, but he doesn't kill anyone who's on my good side. Why don't you have your water and think about that when we make the rest of this ride. And think quick because we don't have far to go."

# Chapter Thirty-Seven

By the time Clint was brought back to the cart, everything was loaded and ready to go. One of the horses was hitched to the front, the gear was stowed and even Sven was tucked away in the back like so much luggage. Clint and Eclipse were taken to the cart and prepared for the ride as well. The Darley Arabian was carefully hitched next to the other animal so he could help pull the cart and a third horse was tied to the side of the cart as a spare. Compared to the amount of attention paid to Eclipse, Clint might as well have been a trunk that nobody wanted to bring along in the first place.

After being trussed up, thrown into the back of the cart and tied to the iron ring embedded in the floor, Clint said, "What a lovely bunch of people."

"Honestly?" Sven asked.

Clint looked over to the other man and held his gaze for a tense couple of seconds. Finally, Sven shrunk back and said, "I suppose that was a stupid question."

"I've heard worse."

"So . . . what did you talk about?"

"Doesn't matter," Clint replied. "It was all just more babble coming from a crazy woman."

"Is that what you think? That they're all crazy?"

Clint settled into a spot with his back against the wall of the cart and his legs stretched as much as possible in front of him. The horses started pulling and the cart rocked back and forth. "Of course they're crazy. What else should I think?"

"Isn't there some part of you that might want to take them up on their offer?"

"No." After a few seconds, Clint sighed and shrugged. "I don't know. Perhaps. Sometimes a man's got to go along with the tide or be swept under."

"That's what I was thinking. But a man's also got to keep an eye on his best interests. What happened if you changed your mind?"

"About what?"

"About following the tide."

"What are you asking me, exactly?"

Sven shrugged his shoulders. "What if you just went along with what they wanted until the time is right?"

"Now that would be an awfully sneaky thing to do, don't you think?"

"Depends on if it goes over well or not."

Clint draped his arms over his bent knees and studied Sven carefully. "I may be mistaken, but it sounds to me like you're plotting something."

"Wouldn't you expect me to be plotting something from the moment I got captured?"

"I would, if you weren't in such pleasant company the whole time. I mean, why would anyone want to escape a couple of bright conversationalists like me and Hall?"

The two of them looked at each other for a second. Clint kept a straight face and Sven didn't seem to know whether or not he'd stuck his foot in his mouth. When Clint cracked a fraction of a smile, Sven let down his guard and started to laugh.

"You almost had me there," Sven said.

"Sometimes there's not much else for a man to do other than laugh at things."

"Sure. But we don't have much time to amuse ourselves."

"What do you mean?" Clint asked.

"Just that there's no telling how long it'll be before this cart is stopped again and . . . well . . . lord only knows what might happen then."

"True enough."

For the next couple of minutes, the only sound within the cart was the echo of the wheels grinding against the road and the thumping rhythm of hooves beating the ground. A wind blew through the warped boards of the cart's walls, making a ghostly whistle that slowly faded away.

Sven held his arms in front of him much like Clint. Since their wrists were bound in a similar fashion, they didn't really have much choice. "So," he said. "Do you think you could take Howlett?"

"That's hard to say. Especially since I barely know him."

"But you must know if you could take him."

"Why do you ask? There are plenty of others in this group to worry about."

"But Howlett seems like the toughest one," Sven said. "If you could take him, then you could take them all, right?"

Clint furrowed his brow as if he was mulling over the proposition. Then he said, "I suppose that makes sense. But men like Howlett don't worry me."

"Really? Why not?"

"Because they're not the ones you need to worry about. The ones that pose a bigger threat are the sneaky little rats who get in close so they can stab you when your back's turned."

Sven looked mildly confused.

"They might even go so far as to pretend to be a prisoner," Clint continued, "and act scared or weak just to keep an eye on you, feel you out, find your strengths and weaknesses, waiting for a good time to make their move."

Sven no longer looked confused. Everything about him changed in the space of one second. First he was huddled over and gazing at Clint with frightened puppy dog eyes. Then he was sitting up straight, glaring at him like a child that was getting ready to crush a spider beneath his foot.

"The thing about these little rats that make them so dangerous," Clint continued, "is how convincing they can be. Even after you sniff one out, you may never be certain about how, exactly, it got there."

"What are you saying?" Sven asked.

Leaning forward a bit, Clint replied, "I know you're not just some idiot who was caught in the wrong place at the wrong time."

"What makes you think that?"

"I'm not an idiot, that's why." A sly grin eased across Clint's face. "Or maybe you're just not as smart as you think you are."

# Chapter Thirty-Eight

Sven made a fist and knocked against the front wall of the cart. Immediately upon hearing that, the driver pulled back on his reins and brought the team to a halt. The Chinese man with the long beard and mustache was the one who opened the door. He had a gun in his hand which he aimed at Clint at the first opportunity.

"Get me out of here," Sven said. When the Chinese man paused for a moment, Sven barked, "Now!"

After that, the Chinese man couldn't move fast enough. He untied Sven from his ropes and even helped him down from the cart. As soon as he was out, Sven started issuing orders. Clint tried to listen in on what was being said, but the task was difficult after the cart was closed up again. Outside, hushed voices and quick footsteps surrounded the cart. Clint stayed put until the cart was opened once again.

"Well?" he said. "Am I going to get the grand treatment too?"

Although Clint wasn't expecting anyone to follow through on that, he wasn't expecting to be pulled partway out of the cart and flipped onto his side so his back was to the open end. He most definitely wasn't expecting a clubbing blow to the back of his head, which was exactly what he got.

***

When he woke up again, he was sitting on the ground against a rock with his hands tied behind his back. At first, he thought a blindfold was tied over his eyes again. After a few blinks, he realized the darkness around him was due to a lack of sunlight.

"How long," he croaked. Clint's throat was scratchy and his entire body ached. He filled his lungs with air, licked his lips and tried again. "How long was I out this time?"

"Most of the day," a smooth, familiar voice replied.

Clint had to turn and crane his neck to get a look at the one who'd answered him. When he did, he not only saw Andrea, but also spotted a pair of campfires flickering about thirty yards away. The cart was parked near the fires and the horses were hitched there as well. Once Clint spotted Eclipse drinking from a large bucket of water, he relaxed a little.

"That stallion has spirit," Andrea said. "Almost too much for his own good."

"What's that supposed to mean?" Clint asked.

Moving in closer to him, Andrea lowered herself to her knees so she could look straight into Clint's face without looming above him. "He nearly proved to be too much to handle," she said. "When we first got him, he was wild as can be."

"So you were one of the thieves that took him?"

"No. All of us in the core group share most everything. It's always 'we' and 'us'."

"How beautiful," Clint grunted.

"I suppose none of us really believe it, though. After all, we are a bunch of thieves. Howlett's the one with the knack for sneaking in and making off with anything on four legs before anyone's the wiser. Don't feel bad that he got yours away from you, either. He once took half a dozen cavalry horses straight out of an Army corral without raising a single alarm. He would've gotten away with more if it wasn't for some corporal who wandered out that way to take a piss. At least, that's how he tells it."

"I'm sure he's told you a lot of things."

"So you think he's all just talk?"

"Not at all," Clint replied. "He strikes me as the sort of man who likes to back up what he says."

"So is Farraday," Andrea said. She scooted closer to him and reached out to tug on the front of Clint's shirt.

"Tell me. How long did you know he was pretending to be your prisoner?"

"If I revealed that sort of information, it might take away some of the wonder. Isn't that what life is all about?"

Andrea smiled and positioned herself so she was straddling Clint's legs. "What if I offered you something in return?"

"What do you have to offer? How about setting me free and giving me my horse?"

"That's already on the table."

"Right. How about doing those things without making me ride with a bunch of lunatics headed for the edge of a cliff?"

"Is that how you see us?" she asked through a little pout.

"Not at all. You're revolutionaries," Clint said. "Trail blazers. Forward thinkers. Now cut me loose."

Andrea clearly wasn't buying Clint's thinly veiled attempt at appeasement. Instead, she was clearly distracted by something else. Her hands hand wandered down the front of his body and were making their way to his groin. "What if I had something else to offer?"

"In return for what?"

She rubbed the growing bulge in Clint's jeans while leaning forward to whisper, "Let's just call it my way of showing how much I appreciate you taking Farraday down a few pegs. If we work together, we could take over this whole operation."

"What profit is there in that?"

"Later," Andrea said. "Or would you rather talk business now?"

Clint could think of a few more matters to discuss, but his body was sending a different message. At the moment, that second message was taking precedence.

# Chapter Thirty-Nine

The others who'd ridden with the cart were sharing one of the campfires in the distance, but might as well have been miles away. Although the air was a bit colder in the darkness Clint was sharing with Andrea, that became less of a problem once she'd crawled on top of him. The chill night air bit into his bare skin when Andrea unbuttoned Clint's shirt and tugged down his jeans. She stood up and peeled off her own jeans before pulling open her shirt and lowering herself back down. Any cold that might have bothered Clint in those moments was washed away when she took his hard cock deep inside of her.

"So," Clint said in the calmest voice he could manage. "This is one of those gangs that takes advantage of their prisoners?"

Settling on top of him, Andrea shifted her hips and placed her hands flat upon Clint's chest. "Do you want me to stop?" she asked.

"Not at all. I was thinking more along the lines of you untying these ropes so I could fully return the favor."

She smiled and started rocking back and forth. "Nice try, Mister Adams."

"Nice," Clint sighed as he savored the weight of her on top of him and the warm dampness of her pussy gliding along his rigid shaft. "Very nice indeed."

Andrea found a rhythm where she ground her hips against his and moved her entire body at a steady, urgent pace. Every time she took him all the way inside of her, she dug her fingernails into Clint's flesh a little harder. There wasn't much he could do since he was tied up so tightly. At least, that's what Andrea must have thought.

When Clint pumped up into her the first time, she let out a surprised groan. Her eyes fluttered open and she smiled down at him as if she was suddenly afraid of drawing attention from the nearby camp. Her focus narrowed down to a single point, however, once Clint began driving into her again and again.

He strained against his ropes, wanting to grab hold of her with both hands. The longer he was denied, the more he wanted to clench his arms around her and hold her within his grasp while finishing the job she'd started. Judging by the hunger in Andrea's eyes and the sound of her throaty grunts, she wouldn't have minded that one bit. But she wasn't about to set him free. In fact, she seemed to enjoy having him at her mercy for the moment.

"You like that?" she purred.

Clint gritted his teeth.

"You like fucking me, don't you?" she grunted into his ear.

Andrea's body writhed on top of him, her slick pussy lips gripping his cock and sliding all the way down to its base. Once there, she moved her hips in a slow circle while digging her fingers through his hair and grabbing his head in her hands. She stared into his eyes and when his gaze drifted down, she arched her back and allowed him to bury his face between her breasts.

At first, Clint kissed her naked skin. Once the salty taste of her sweat mingled with the flavor of Andrea's skin, he kissed her harder and nipped at her flesh. She laughed quietly and held him closer. Her hips were now pumping in time to Clint's upward thrusts.

Andrea's nipples grew hard in Clint's mouth and when he gently bit them, he could feel her entire body respond. Her muscles tensed and her legs clenched around him even tighter. Once again moving his mouth to the track of skin between her breasts, Clint licked all the way up to her neck which caused Andrea to sit upright astride him. Rather than stay in one spot for too long, she leaned back and supported her weight on both hands.

Now that she was in a similar position as Clint, Andrea spread her legs open wide and moved her hips in a steady, pulsing beat. Both she and Clint stared straight across at each other, their bodies moving in time to a rhythm that flowed naturally through them. All he had to do was look down and Clint could see his thick erection driving between her glistening lips. Soon, Andrea reached down to rub her pussy, her fingers quickly centering on the little pink nub of her clit.

Her fingers moved faster as Clint pumped harder. Before long, Andrea kept her body mostly still so she could enjoy the pleasure that was surging through her. Clint enjoyed watching her approach her climax, but was quickly distracted by what was building up inside of his own body.

Andrea's face took on a primal expression. She slid her fingers down so she could not only feel herself but could also feel the spot where Clint impaled her. He slid in one more time, eased out and then pounded all the way into her. Andrea might have cried out as she climaxed, but she didn't have enough breath to make a sound. Instead, she sat up straight and arched her back, giving Clint a perfect view of her bare breasts and pert nipples.

When her orgasm subsided, her entire body trembled in a way that Clint could feel all the way down to his toes. That was enough to push him over the edge and soon he exploded inside of her.

Andrea leaned forward again, much like a drooping plant that covered his body with hers. Keeping him inside of her, she writhed slowly and placed her mouth close to Clint's.

"You see?" she whispered. "We fit awfully well together."

"That is a good point," he admitted. "And one I can't exactly argue with."

"You think about what I offered." Andrea stood up and slowly pulled her clothes back on. Leaving her shirt mostly unbuttoned and her jeans slung low on her hips, she said, "I'll just give you some time to think it over."

"And what happens if I refuse your generous offer?" Clint asked. "No more nightly visits like this one?"

"That's right. Also, there's a real good chance that you'll be cut into several pieces before being scattered beneath the next tree we decide to use as a landmark."

Despite the threat that was made and the knowledge that it could be carried out against him, Clint had a tough time being upset with Andrea's words. He was still reeling from being inside her and savoring the sight of her walking away.

# Chapter Forty

Clint was glad to be left alone at first. As the minutes ticked away, however, he started to wonder if he was foolish for being optimistic in the first place. Before he could lose hope, he heard the scrape of cautious footsteps approaching him from the shadows nearby.

"Psst. Hey, Adams. You awake?"

"No, Jarred," Clint replied. "I was just so comfortable here against this rock that I dozed off for a spell."

"Well if you like, I can come back some other time."

"Get over here, damn you."

Hall crawled on his belly so that most of his body was covered by some dry brush on the outermost edge of the little clearing. He reached out to grab Clint's bound wrists with one hand and start sawing at the rope using the knife he held in his other hand. "Whoever these guys are waiting for," he said while working, "isn't anywhere close to this camp. I've been tracking you since you were dragged out of that cathouse in camp and—"

"You've been tracking me the entire time?" Clint snapped.

"Yeah. Isn't that why you wanted to ride along with me? I'm a damn good tracker."

"I was hoping you would've done something before I was taken out of camp."

"And I was hoping you wouldn't have gotten knocked cold," Hall said. "Seems like we don't always get what we want."

"You were also supposed to keep an eye on Don," Clint reminded him. "Where might that one be?"

Not only had Hall stopped talking, but he'd stopped cutting as well. For a moment, Clint wondered if the bounty hunter had slithered off somewhere else. Eventually, a voice drifted through the air that was barely loud enough to be heard.

"He's dead," Hall said.

"What?"

"Don's dead. He didn't make it out of the cathouse. One of the girls said he was shot dead by the fella you were looking after. Sven."

"His name's Farraday," Clint said.

The next sounds Clint heard were the scraping of Hall's arms and legs against the ground as he crawled around to look into Clint's eyes when he asked, "Are you joking?"

"Nope."

"How the hell do you know that? Did he tell you?"

"I figured it out."

"How?" Hall asked.

"Will you just get back to work?"

"Keep your voice down, you fool. There are armed men nearby and they're looking over here. I don't think they saw me, but it doesn't help matters if you draw attention to yourself."

Clint looked toward the camp. One of the fires was still being tended, but the other had died down to nothing but a pile of flickering embers. The only people he could make out distinctly were the Chinese man with the long hair and the larger fellow who had the face that resembled a long stretch of rough road. Everyone else was either in the shadows or sleeping in their bedrolls. The Chinese man was on his feet patrolling the area closest to the dying fire. He looked over to Clint and stared him down from a distance. At that moment, Clint swore he could see that man's hands tightening around the rifle he held.

"See what you did?" Hall whispered. "That one's gonna come over here."

"What I did?" Clint hissed under his breath. "You're the one who came over here."

"Would you rather I left you?"

"Of course not. Just keep still."

Hall did as he was told, keeping his chest and belly flat against the ground. His head was resting on its side, making him look like an Indian listening for footfalls in an open stretch of desert. Although the Chinese guard seemed intrigued by something he'd spotted in Clint's vicinity, he didn't seem to have spotted anything worth making the trip all the way over to check on him.

"He doesn't see you," Clint said quietly while giving the distant guard an upward nod.

"And why would he bother checking on you?" Hall said from his spot on the ground. "If the rest of the camp chose to ignore you while you and the lady were—"

"I hope you were doing something more than hanging back and watching me with Andrea," Clint scolded. "I thought it went without saying that I figured if one of us got captured that the other would come after him. That's what a partnership is."

"No need to tell me, Adams. I was scouting the camp and looking for any reinforcements that might have been on the way. I was also waiting for a good chance to get in close and free you. If you weren't so intent on keeping that traitorous whore so close, I might have been able to do something a little sooner. Then again, it doesn't seem like they're too concerned with watching you."

Clint sighed. "They're giving me time to think about joining up with them."

"Well?"

"Well what?"

"What's your decision on that?" Hall asked.

"Do I even need to dignify that with a response?"

"Nah, I do have a better question for you, though."

"What is it?"

"How'd you know about Sven?"

Grudgingly, Clint admitted, "I didn't. Not right away. Even when I woke up from taking that knock to the head, I thought Don was the man I was after since he was the last one I saw. But Sven was the one who was in that cart with me when I came to and he didn't have a scratch on him."

"Doesn't prove anything," Hall said.

"Whenever those men came along to check our ropes or pull us out of that cart, they seemed to handle Sven like a piece of fine china while knocking me around without a care in the world."

"I can't really blame them for that."

Ignoring the bounty hunter's snide comments, Clint continued sifting through his thoughts. "But it wasn't until he started questioning me about how I might match up against Howlett. He tried to pass it off like he was concerned, but he was more curious about figuring out my strategy or, more importantly, any weakness I might be worried about."

"That does seem strange," Hall said.

"I know it's not conclusive, but none of it sat right with me. He just seemed a bit too anxious to get me to talk when a man in his position should have been more concerned with just getting the hell out of there." In the end, Clint had to admit, "A lot of it boiled down to gut instinct though."

"It usually does. So, you eventually got him to say who he was?"

"Not as such," Clint replied. "He admitted to trying to pull the wool over my eyes and digging for information. As for him being Farraday . . ."

"Let me guess. Another hunch?"

"They've served me well this far."

Once again working on the ropes, Hall said, "You've got more hunches than a camel."

"Humps."

"What?"

"Camels have humps, not hunches. Actually," Clint quickly added, "I don't give a damn about camels. Just keep cutting."

# Chapter Forty-One

"All right," Hall said when his blade severed the rope binding Clint's wrists. "You're free. Let's get the hell out of here."

"Not yet."

"Why not? Them others are either asleep, tending to the fire or talking among themselves."

Clint squinted at the largest cluster of figures in the distance. There was half a dozen of them all huddled near the cart. "That's definitely Farraday," Clint said.

"So what if it is?"

"The other men acted differently around him. Even Andrea seemed to treat him differently somehow and she prides herself on being the one to give orders instead of taking them."

"That don't answer my question, Adams."

"You said it yourself. Nobody else is coming. It just makes sense that a small group of revolutionaries would have to keep moving rather than stay in one spot where they could be picked off. That way, they can spread all the savagery and fear they want while most everyone thinks they're a bunch of demons in the night."

"Revolutionaries?"

"That's what they fancy themselves to be, anyhow," Clint told him. "I was given a sales pitch to try and get me to sign on with them. This bunch supposedly wants to take New Mexico for themselves."

Sheathing his knife, Hall reached for a spare Smith & Wesson pistol that was tucked under his gun belt at the small of his back. "That's insane."

"Maybe. Maybe not."

"If that's what you think, then you've lost your damn mind and I don't intend on being dragged down with you."

Clint turned to face him while rubbing his wrists to get the blood flowing through them once more. "Think about it! From everything we've heard, this group is basically a collection of outlaws and killers looking to make some fast money and raise some hell. The only ones with their sights set any higher than that are probably the three at the center of it all."

"You think that's all this outfit is? Three folks corralling a bunch of gunhands?"

"Why not?"

"Because," Hall said, "it would take a lot more than that to take over an entire state."

"Most likely, that's just the goods they're trying to sell to anyone who'll listen. Odds are a lot better that they've just got some sort of scheme cooked up to extort money from landowners, run the law out of a couple of counties or just make themselves look like the devil himself so folks will be too scared to stand against them when they come around to rob them."

Chuckling, Hall said, "Oh, is that all?"

"If there was a larger group to worry about, I'd be more concerned with whatever their plan might be," Clint explained. "But I honestly think this is the heart of the operation right here."

The bounty hunter was still on his belly to avoid being spotted from afar. "So you think all of what we've seen and heard about just comes from some of these men here in this camp?"

"What we've seen may be terrible, but it's not something that would take an army to accomplish. It's basically just a bunch of little fires that were set across a wide area that have spread into something bigger."

"I suppose that could be."

"If there was more of an organization at work, there would have to be a structure of some kind. This is all a bunch of smoke, blood and big talk."

"Those trees are a lot more than just smoke."

"They're just trees, Jarred. Trees and bodies. If either of us traded away our souls, we could make plenty of those same trees ourselves."

Hall shuddered at that prospect.

Suddenly, Clint snapped his fingers. "Think of these men as weeds."

"Huh?"

"When you see a weed, it's this huge tangled mess of snarled leaves, stems and whatnot that forms a thick . . ."

"I've seen weeds, Adams, get to the point. Some of those gunmen by that fire are taking an interest in you."

Clint took a quick look in that direction to find that some of the men there were indeed watching him a bit closer. They weren't rushing over with guns blazing, which meant they must not have spotted Hall just yet. Even so, it was only a matter of time before that situation changed.

"My point is that the mess on top doesn't matter when it comes to a weed. All that does matter is the root and more often than not, those roots are awfully small. The trick is just finding them and cutting them at the source."

One of the men from the campfire shouted something at him, but Clint ignored the other man's words.

"Are you proposing that we clear out the weeds from this here garden?" Hall asked.

"It's either that or sit around and wait for them to do what they like with us."

"Ain't no us, Adams. Far as they know, I'm not even here."

"So you'd rather skin out of here and let these mad dogs kill however many more just to spread fear and make a few more dollars?" Clint asked.

"Hey!" the man near the fire shouted. "What's going on over there? Is someone with you?"

Both Clint and Hall kept their heads down. "After the insanity these men have caused," Clint said, "they've got to be fairly well known in these parts."

"That's usually the point," Hall said.

"And there's bound to be someone willing to pay a healthy sum to anyone who puts an end to them."

Hall's eyebrows rose. "You've got a point there."

"Plus, it's not very likely that we could just ride away from this mess," Clint said. "Not without having to fight our way out of at least one or two ambushes along the way. Murderers tend to be awfully vengeful."

"Eh, save the sales pitch," Hall grunted. "I was sold when you mentioned the healthy sum of reward money."

## Chapter Forty-Two

The main campfire was slowly dying, which allowed more shadows to creep in on all sides. As he approached the rock where Clint was sitting, the Chinese gunman held his rifle in a loose grip.

"Shut your mouth," the gunman said. "If you have something to say, wait until morning."

At that moment, Hall lifted his Remington and fired a shot that caught the Chinese outlaw in the chest. The gunman staggered backward, only to be knocked down by a second bullet that drilled a hole within an inch of the first.

"I don't think he saw you," Clint said as he got to his feet and rushed forward to search the Chinese man's body.

Hall replaced the spent rounds in his pistol. "There's nothing like starting off on the right foot. If you want to argue about it, I suggest you wait. This evening's festivities are just beginning."

The rifle that the Chinese man had been carrying was a Winchester. As soon as Clint picked it up, he checked to make sure it was loaded and put it to work. At least three gunmen from the sputtering campfire were responding to the shots that had been fired. The rest of the camp had been stirred up as well, but not all of the outlaws were about to charge into the fight head-on.

Clint sighted along the top of the Winchester, waiting for a target to present itself. He didn't have to wait long before one of the outlaws running toward him opened fire with a pistol. Lead burned through the air above Clint's head which did nothing to rattle the man behind the Winchester. Clint let out a slow breath, squeezed the rifle's trigger and put a round through the gunman's heart.

After levering in a fresh round, Clint took aim at the next closest man who was already shooting at him and Hall. The Winchester spat another plume of sparks to send the outlaw with the gnarled face and long hair to an early grave.

"We've got some men circling around on us," Hall warned.

"Circling to which side?" Clint asked.

After firing a few quick shots to send a pair of men running for cover, Hall said, "Take your pick."

"We're dead if we stay here with only a rock and some bushes to hide behind."

"What else would you suggest?"

"There's only one other option." With that, Clint held the Winchester in one hand and drew the Smith &

Wesson he'd been given with the other. Setting his sights on the largest group of outlaws, Clint marched forward and started shooting.

There weren't many things that could catch Jarred Hall off guard anymore, but that was one of them. He quickly set aside any reservations he might have had and drew a little .38 he kept in an ankle holster. "And here I thought he was the smart one," the bounty hunter said. Shrugging, he added, "Guess it don't make much difference at this point." He then let out a wild yell that would make a Comanche proud and commenced firing with both hands.

Even without the bounty hunter to back his play, Clint would have done a fair amount of damage. Two of the remaining outlaws were in his sights, having been caught trying to sneak up on Clint's right. They started firing as soon as they saw him point the Winchester in their direction, but their shots were hurried and flew wide of their target. Clint took his time and did the job right, knocking both men to the dirt as easy as blasting tin cans from a fence post.

Hall found the other pair of men who'd attempted to get around on the other side of them. After a shout bout of shooting stopped, Clint called out, "You still breathing?"

"Yeah," the bounty hunter replied.

"Need any help?"

"Just a moment." After a few seconds, another shot cracked through the air and Hall said, "Nah. I'm good." There was a lot less movement near the campfires. The one that was still flickering showed Clint nothing but the horses that had been tethered to some thick roots. Eclipse was among them and appeared to be unharmed, so he turned his attention elsewhere. Although the second campfire had been doused some time ago, there were more than just shadows creeping amid the smoke that hung in the air.

"Farraday!" Clint shouted. "This madness ends right here and now. Show yourself while there's still time to get out of here with your life."

After a few seconds, a voice behind Clint said, "Did you really expect that to work?"

"Not really," Clint said to Hall. "But it was worth a try."

"I've got a better idea."

"Then by all means, I'd like to hear it."

"We're placing the lot of you under arrest!" Hall announced. "And if you don't toss your weapons down, we'll know that this whole revolution of yours ain't nothing but a bunch of idiotic talk from a group of bloodthirsty animals."

"What do you know about revolution?" hollered the man Clint had known as Sven. He stepped out from behind the cart holding a pistol in each hand.

"I'll be damned," Clint whispered. "That did work."

"I get hunches too, you know," Hall said.

# Chapter Forty-Three

With every step he took, the lanky figure who'd been hiding behind the cart walked taller. "Do you know who I am?" he shouted. "I'm Martin Farraday!"

"Never heard of you," Hall replied. "Not unless you count the times I heard a name mentioned in passing."

"Don't worry if you don't recognize it right away," Clint said. "Men like him want nothing more than to be legends and it's always easier to just act like you're already one instead of doing anything to earn it."

"I've earned plenty," Farraday said.

Clint stepped forward as well, gauging the distance between him and any potential targets. As far as he could tell, there was only Farraday and one other man who was on one knee peeking around the cart. That one had a rifle propped against his shoulder, but had yet to fire a shot. Even from a distance, Clint could tell that man was rattled all the way down to his core.

"What have you done that's so great?" Clint asked. "Slaughtered a bunch of innocents? Hung some outlaws from a few trees? If that's all it took, then every lynch mob in the country would have already staked a claim to fame."

Hall chimed in by saying, "I never thought of it that way. This whole gang is just one big lynch mob. They might talk a lot louder, but that about sums it up."

Seeing how every word was burrowing under Farraday's skin, Clint kept the ball rolling. "Oh, but let's not forget the horses. They're real good at stealing horses too."

"There was more to it than that and you know it!" Farraday snarled.

"Actually I don't. I would never have heard of you if one of your men hadn't taken my horse in the dead of night like the damn coward he is."

This time, Clint's words hit another target than Farraday. He was grateful for that because Howlett emerged from a shadow less than twenty yards away from him, Clint hadn't even known he was there.

"Only reason you woke up at all instead of getting your damn throat cut," Howlett said, "was because I was only getting paid for yer horse."

"You're too shortsighted to see the whole picture," Farraday said. "Claiming bounties on horse thieves is easier money than pulling gold out of a river or carrying it out of a bank. Those men come to me with those horses and I've got plenty of places to sell the animals for a tidy profit. If I don't have a use for those men in my cause, I hand them over for an even bigger profit so they can be disposed of by the authorities. If I want to spread my word to the people in this state or others, I hang them from one of my trees. And on the rare occasion that someone brings a truly magnificent animal to me, I can keep them in my personal stable where they can be used by my men."

"Sounds like a pretty good system," Hall said. "Except for one part."

"Which part is that?"

"This moment right here," Clint said.

Hall nodded and grinned. "Took the words right out of my mouth."

Howlett shook his head. "This moment doesn't mean a damn thing. We'll kill you, ride into another county and gather up another bunch of men looking to join up with us. By now, all we gotta do is show our faces in a saloon or two before we get volunteers wanting to ride with us."

"Normally, I prefer to give a man a chance to do the right thing," Clint said. "But I can tell you're not the sort who would just throw down his guns and come peacefully."

"He's a horse thief, Adams," Hall said. "Most likely, he's afraid of most men and women. That's why he can only feel like a bad man around an animal."

Howlett made a guttural sound that came from the back of his throat and exploded from him with fiery rage. Not only did he raise his pistol to fire a shot at Clint, but he charged forward like a bull. Clint reflexively took a shot at him, aiming his gun as if he was pointing his finger. His round caught Howlett in the upper torso, but it was impossible to see exactly where because he was still charging.

Clint fired again, missing this time with the unfamiliar gun, since Howlett had shifted to a lower stance and pushed off with both legs to throw himself at him. He may have been shorter than Clint, but Howlett's frame was thick with muscle. When he made contact, his bulk was enough to bring Clint down. Howlett landed on top of him and any help that might have been forthcoming from Hall would have to wait, since the bounty hunter was trading shots with at least one other man.

Every one of Clint's muscles tensed against an onslaught of blows including heavy punches, wild kicks, and even a few head butts. Instead of trying to beat the wild man at his own game, Clint focused on two simple tasks. He kept his head down and brought one knee up toward his chest.

Howlett snarled like an animal, pausing only to draw a breath and pull a knife from a sheath hanging from his belt. Clint had no doubt the smaller man was a true craftsman with that blade. By the time Howlett brought the blade up over his head in preparation of a downward strike, Clint had gotten his leg between them so he could push the other man away. Howlett spat a few obscenities as he was tossed back. Before he could scramble close enough to cut Clint open with the knife in his hand, Clint's pistol barked twice to punch two messy holes through Howlett's face.

As he stood up, Clint was ready to shoot Howlett again. But all the smaller man could do was twitch on his side as his life trickled out of him. Nearby, Hall was standing over another body and reloading his Remington.

"Is that Farraday?" Clint asked.

"Yep," Hall replied. He then stooped down to take something from the dead man's hand. "I think this belongs to you." With that, he tossed what he'd taken through the air.

Recognizing the modified Colt before it reached his hand, Clint caught it and examined the pistol. "Looks undamaged, at least."

"The little prick didn't get a chance to use it. Seeing as how I came to rescue you, I'd say you owe me."

"What did you have in mind?"

# Chapter Forty-Four

There were a good number of bodies scattered about that camp that were worth something to any bounty hunter. Fortunately for Hall, he not only had a cart to carry them all, but an extra set of indebted hands to help with the lifting. In a short amount of time, Hall was driving the cart slowly down the trail headed back to the Texas border.

Clint rode Eclipse alongside the cart. "How far do you intend to go?" he asked.

"Tonight? Not far. Just enough to put some distance between us and that camp. You know, just in case there were any stragglers on their way to meet up with the rest of them idiots."

"I didn't see Andrea's body in that pile."

"That's right," Hall replied. "I guess she was the brains of the outfit since she knew when to cut and run. There was one other fella, too. Didn't recognize him, so it ain't worth hunting him down. Besides, the money I collect from bringing in Howlett alone will be enough to buy me a nice little piece of land."

"Where might that land be?"

"Somewhere quiet. Why, Adams? You worried I won't give you your share?"

"Not hardly. Just thought it might be good to check in on you every now and then. Men attached to a movement like this tend to be fanatical. I'd hate to think any of them came looking for some measure of revenge."

Hall spat out a hearty laugh. "I've had more organized movements in a shit house. You were right about one thing, at least. These men were crazy, pure and simple."

"Lots of crazy men throughout history have done plenty of damage. Given a bit more time, these may have cut a real swath across New Mexico."

"Instead, they'll fade away like the other outlaw gangs who were put down like rabid dogs," Hall said.

Clint nodded. "I suppose so." After a few seconds, he added, "I've got to admit. I'm surprised you were able to bait both Farraday and Howlett into jumping at us the way you did."

"It's just a matter of saying the right thing in the right tone. Really annoys the living shit out of people, you know?"

"Yeah. You've got a real talent for that."

Hall smiled and then scowled. "Hey! What do you mean by that?"

"Nothing. Nothing at all."